Cover design by Julia Gerbach

ISBN 9798990252288 (paperback)

ISBN 9798990252271 (ebook)

www.katherinegrantromance.com

Also by Katherine Grant

The Countess Chronicles:

The Ideal Countess
New Year's Masquerade
The Duchess Wager
The Husband Plot

The Prestons:

The Baron Without Blame

The Viscount Without Virtue

The Governess Without Guilt

The Charmer Without a Cause

The Sailor Without a Sweetheart

The Countess Without Conviction

The Miss Without a Mister

The Widower Without a Will

Northfield Hall Novellas

(an unordered series for the mood reader)

The Hellion of Drury Lane

It's In Her Kiss

Three Nights With Her Husband

Letters to Her Love

In The Wide Open Light

Her Perfect Pirate

Plus, a free short story, The Spinster, available exclusively at www.katherinegrantromance.com

What to Expect from The Widower Without a Will

This secret love affair risks nothing except his legacy—and her heart.

Lord **Martin Preston is not looking for love.** All he wants is to secure his legacy as a progressive baron and caring father. When the rector's widow needs a place to stay, he doesn't think twice before offering her a room at Northfield Hall.

Martha Bellamy lives in shadows. For a decade, she has been under the cloud of scandal around her son's demise, and now she must also live in the darkness of her husband's death. **Enchanted by Lord**

Preston, Martha volunteers to be his private secretary—and, she hopes, his new private friend.

Martin didn't know how much he craved a confidante like Martha. **Yet as they share more and more of their hearts with each other, he cannot forget she is a poor widow in his care, not a woman he can love.** When tragedy strikes, Martin finds himself doing everything he can in order to protect all he has worked for—and he must decide whether Martha is included in his legacy.

In this final installment of The Prestons, Martin reckons with the legend of Northfield Hall and must prove once and for all whether he deserves the reputation he has earned.

This story touches on themes of deep grief. For content advisories, please visit www.katherinegrantromance. com/contentadvisories.

The Widower Without a Will

Katherine Grant

In writing this story, I hold close the memories of Marilyn and Nathan.

CHAPTER ONE

AUGUST 1823

ON A BEAUTIFUL SUMMER day, Lord Martin Preston had no right to feel sorrow, yet his heart hung heavy as he drove his gig through Thatcham, the village that looked always the same yet was ever changing. How many times, in the course of his sixty-two years, had he ridden down Chapel Street? The same buildings with the same white plaster walls and the same thatched roofs sprouted up from the soft hills of the countryside.

But the people inside them were different. The baker who had been a young man when Martin was a boy now lay in the graveyard under a respectable marker, while his great-grandson kept the village in fresh bread. The shop that had once been a haberdasher's had since been a stationer's, a grocer's, and now a tailor's. The old barn that had sat empty in Martin's youth now stood proudly as a school for the village children.

And his dear friend Maulvi now lay in a sickbed when once he had walked daily from Thatcham to Northfield Hall and back.

At least he and Maulvi had spent a nice afternoon together. Though he was confined to bed, Maulvi was in fine spirits, and they had read a letter from Martin's son Nate, gotten into a debate about whether slavery would ever be abolished in Britain's colonies, and reminisced about when they were both three decades younger and optimistic about the world.

Then the Widow Croft had eased into the room with a bowl of broth and a basin of hot water, apologizing to Martin. "I had better give Mr. Maulvi his wash now, sir."

Strange, how Martin still thought of her as the Widow Croft when she and Maulvi had lived as common-law husband and wife since before Martin himself had married. If they had both been Christians, she would be Mrs. Maulvi. If she were of the same class as Martin, he might have asked her permission to call her by her first name—whatever it was.

Martin supposed his children would accuse him of having an inflexible mind, since in all these years it had never occurred to him to change how he thought of her. She was the Widow Croft; it didn't matter what Martin called her in his head so long as she remained Maulvi's dear partner and lover.

These ruminations kept him company as he guided the gig down Chapel Street, back towards Northfield Hall. He lifted his hand periodically to acknowledge the pedestrians greeting him, but he barely saw them, his mind turning as it so often did on thoughts that kept him away from the mundane.

Then—a flash of golden hair caught his eye. By instinct, he knew it to be his daughter Caroline, and he slowed the horse before he even consciously realized he had seen her.

Things had not been right with Caroline for years. Not since Martin had tried to prevent her from marrying Eddie Chow. Before, he had been her hero; ever since, she looked at him as if he were a snake who at any moment might bite her ankle. No matter that Martin had apologized and admitted his mistakes. At least they had semi-regular dinners where they both tried desperately to make conversation that would not upset each other.

At the moment, Caroline stood outside the pub in conversation with two other women: the publican's wife and the late rector's widow. As Martin watched, Caroline shepherded the women into the shade, and her gentle words—"You see, my dear Mrs. Bellamy, there are plenty of options for you to consider"—carried in the afternoon breeze.

Mrs. Bellamy, the widow, did not look convinced. She was a woman of roughly Martin's age with silver hair tied in a simple knot beneath her black bonnet, a white complexion that had over the years grown tan, and a softly rounded body that demanded no notice. Martin had met her a handful of times in the decade that her husband was rector, in the same capacity that he had met almost everyone in Thatcham a handful of times in his forty-odd years as the local baron, which meant he knew her mostly in terms of the stories that reached his ears. Practical, community-minded, never shirking in her duties to the poor, ill, or aged.

He knew of the terrible tragedy of her life, the one that had driven her husband to seek the living in Thatcham, but he liked to assume the worst details had been exaggerated.

Martin pulled his horse to a stop and, descending from the gig, tied him to the pub's hitching post. Of the three women, Mrs. Bellamy saw him first and took a step backward from their circle, as if he were an invading army who demanded retreat.

"Good afternoon," Martin said as warmly as possible. He couldn't help but touch a hand to Caroline's shoulder—a father's instinct to check that his child was, in fact, still there. "I am driving home to Northfield Hall and wondered if I could be of help with whatever troubles you."

The publican's wife, at least, looked happy to see him. She was in the generation between Martin and Caroline, perhaps in her forties, and no doubt had her hands full keeping the pub in order. "Mrs. Bellamy is seeking somewhere to stay, my lord, but I'm afraid our rooms are all let."

"Seeking somewhere to stay?" A rector's widow did not typically need to take a room in a pub.

"The new rector arrived today," Mrs. Bellamy explained. Martin was surprised to discover her voice was beautiful, like a glass bell ringing in a silent chamber. "There is no room for me to remain at the rectory with his family while I wait to hear from my niece if I may live with her."

As matter-of-factly as she delivered the information, her words quickly painted a picture of the awkward situation. First, the new rector had every legal right to take possession of the house—but it would have been kind to coordinate with Mrs. Bellamy so she might arrange for her own move ahead of time. Second, the late Mr. Bellamy had been deceased for more than six months already, so for Mrs. Bellamy to be without a place to stay indicated either an extraordinary lack of planning or that her family was reluctant to take her in. Third, as everyone pretended not to know, that family was small because her only child had died at his own hand, leaving Mrs. Bellamy at the mercy of her niece.

And fourth—perhaps the most crucial element in his daughter's eyes—this was all Martin's fault, since he was the one who had appointed the new rector.

It was his legal obligation. If he hadn't done so, then the bishop would have. It was not as if Martin had thought, *I would like to make a widow homeless today.* Yet he had selected the Reverend Mr. Sebright from the pool of candidates—primarily as a favor to Lord Harewood, who had in turn voted with Martin for gaol reform—which meant *he* was responsible for the inconsiderate rector turning poor Mrs. Bellamy onto the street.

"Of course, Mr. Chow and I would take you in," said Caroline, triggering in Martin a second of bewilderment before he remembered she did not refer to his carpenter Mr. Yin Chow but to the son, Eddie, to whom Caroline was now married. "We have only the one bed, however, and our second room is also the kitchen, and

I can't see that you would be comfortable. I'm confident once we take a survey of Thatcham that we will find multiple families who will argue with each other about which one gets the favor of your company."

To her credit, Mrs. Bellamy was a stoic woman. She met the suggestion that the whole village be told of her embarrassing plight with only a pinch of the lips.

Martin touched Caroline's shoulder again. "Surely that isn't necessary."

Caroline turned hot, angry eyes on him. "We aren't going to send Mrs. Bellamy to an inn at Theale where she knows no one as she waits for her niece to send instructions!"

As if, in his simple sentence that had not been a suggestion at all, Martin had resurrected all the evils he had ever visited upon Caroline and insisted she live through them once more.

When, he wondered, would it occur to her that he was just a human, and that his heart could be broken, too?

"Certainly not," he said, and he plastered on his most gracious smile as he turned to Mrs. Bellamy. "It would be my honor if you would make your home at Northfield Hall for as long as you need."

The publican's wife cried out, "Oh, what a wonderful idea, my lord!"

Mrs. Bellamy remained stoic. However, her lips did un-pinch ever so slightly, and her eyes—hazel—met his with a warmth he hadn't yet experienced from her. "If I wouldn't be in your way, sir."

"Indeed, you would be my only company for the foreseeable future, saving me from eating endless suppers on my own."

The wrong thing to say; Caroline would ordinarily have swooped in to correct him that he *wasn't* alone, since someone was making him that supper in the kitchens and someone else was carrying it to him in the dining room (or, more often now, his study), and all he needed to do was invite the servants to eat with him if he wanted company.

But Martin had earned enough favor with her that she did *not* eviscerate him for failing to eradicate the class system in one fell swoop. Instead, she clasped both his elbow and Mrs. Bellamy's. "There, you see, I knew there was no reason to despair! Now, Papa, is there room in the gig for Mrs. Bellamy's things?"

Martin almost said no, expecting Mrs. Bellamy to have a household's worth of belongings, but he saw in a flash that her *things* waited by the front of the pub: one chest, two cloth bags, and a hatbox.

What would it be like, he wondered, to have one's life reduced to so little?

One of the men loitering in the pub came out to load the gig. Martin paid his tip, then helped Mrs. Bellamy up. In that small moment, she proved herself a country woman: her gloved hand was thick in his, her grip sturdy, and she barely needed a boost to get onto the bench. But as she rose past him, he caught a surprising whiff of perfume—a spicy, flowery smell he associated with the excess of London.

Martin tucked away the observation. "Shall you join us for Sunday dinner this week?" he asked Caroline.

She smiled—that fake smile she used with him so often now to pretend that she still thought of him as her beloved father. "You may expect Eddie and me both."

He had meant the collective *you*. Caroline never came without Eddie, as if she were afraid that spending one meal away from him might rend them apart forever. Or perhaps she was afraid her great and terrible father would lock her away if she didn't bring her husband to protect her.

In any case, she had said yes, which meant Martin could resume this dance with her in a few days. He nodded. "Excellent. I'll inform Mrs. Chow."

Caroline smiled. Martin climbed into the gig. Mrs. Bellamy shifted away, so that not even the lace trim of her widow's weeds brushed against his leg.

And there was nothing left to do but spur the horse on through Thatcham, which was always the same and yet ever changing.

MARTHA KNEW BETTER THAN to make small talk with a baron. If he desired to speak to her, he would find a topic of conversation. The last thing she wanted was for him to think she might grab upward at this first real interaction, and so she kept herself to herself as the gig rocked down the dirt road to North-field Hall.

She had only been to the Hall once in her ten years living in Thatcham, and that had been for the wedding of Miss Preston and Eddie Chow. A strange day, that: the ceremony and fol-lowing party had both been in the fields, like a summer festival, and no one—not even her husband, Kenneth—would say how unnatural it was for a baron's daughter to marry a glazier.

Martha had been seized with terrible anger and walked home early, even though it was five miles and she had been wearing her good slippers instead of sturdy boots. When Kenneth had returned at twilight, he waved off her apology, saying no one had noticed her absence—not even him, until the dancing started.

Two years later, and the new Mrs. Chow was still a blush-ing bride, her glazier husband often seen stealing a kiss as they retreated to their small set of rooms that no baron's daughter should rightfully be happy in. To his credit, he worked hard; to *her* credit, she still acted like a lady of the realm as she in-serted herself in this dispute or that and generally helped patch the tears in Thatcham's social fabric. Martha had gotten to know Mrs. Caroline Chow through visits to sickbeds and the new annual Christmas fete to raise parish funds, held in the barn-cum-schoolroom-cum-assembly hall. There was nothing Martha could object to in Mrs. Chow, except that she should have let well enough alone and married someone of her own class.

But Martha knew, too, that her fury did not really have anything to do with Mrs. Chow or God's social order. Like everything else in her life, it came back to Lucas, who would never come home to make things right.

"I feel I should apologize," Lord Preston said as the gig turned from the road onto Northfield Hall's private drive. "I appointed Mr. Sebright to the living while I was still in London, and it did not occur to me to advise you of it nor to ensure you had somewhere to go afterward."

Embarrassment burned her cheeks. She believed Lord Preston's apology was sincere, yet it only served to remind her how poorly she had managed life since—well, at least since Kenneth had died of that horrid cough. "You had no obligation to me. You gave me the full six months to make my preparations. I only regret that those six months were not enough for me and that now you must take me on as your burden."

The truth was that she had been wallowing. Visiting Kenneth's grave each day with a new sprig of flowers. Pleasuring in the fact that at last, she could wear black. Accepting visits and condolence letters and all the rituals of grieving that had been denied her when Lucas died.

She hadn't stopped to think about the fact that she must keep on living until the new rector had been announced.

"You are no burden to me," he said, as anyone gallant would have done. Martha had expected that much of him. She had only met the man a handful of times, but his reputation loomed large in Britain and especially in Thatcham. He had turned Northfield Hall from a typical country estate into a safe haven for anyone destitute or alone, where everyone who labored on the property shared in its profits, and where no imports from the colonial economy—tainted by chattel slavery and other forced labor—were consumed. He was the kind of lord who attended every sitting of Parliament and took up the poor man's plight at great cost to his own reputation.

Even before he had pulled up to the inn, Martha had suspected her homelessness would be solved with a room somewhere on the five hundred acres of Northfield.

That didn't change the fact that she was a burden.

"I am waiting to hear from my niece," Martha assured him, looking at the farmers diligently building hayricks in the field so she didn't have to face the baron. "Her husband has a living in Battersea. They'll have room in the vicarage for an old woman."

She did not tell him of her nephew, who commanded both a rectory and a vicarage near Devon, who had replied to her inquiry with a polite no (*Between my family and my students, dear Aunt, I am afraid there would be no bed for you*). Nor her youngest sister's letter, which had made excuses for herself as well as all three of her children. Her eldest brother had long since passed, but his grandson had proactively written Martha to offer condolences and inform her there was no place for her at his farm.

No one wanted to be tainted by Lucas's scandal. It was why she and Kenneth had been shuffled from Tolpuddle to Thatcham—and why Kenneth had ossified into a man who could bear no imperfections, risk no laughter. People already believed that Lucas hovered over them like a curse; Kenneth reacted by dedicating every moment of his life to proving they were above reproach, despite their son.

Martha had hopes that her niece Georgina, a practical girl for whom she had always had a soft spot, would take her in.

"In the meantime, you shall have your choice of rooms at Northfield Hall," Lord Preston said. Ahead of them, the house began to appear with its odd combination of a Tudor east wing attached to the rest of its red brick. "My children have all relinquished their claims to any specific suite, and for the moment, I have no other houseguests."

He said it with the intonation of an upper-class toff who found everything amusing and nothing important. The tone did not come naturally from him. Martha turned her head ever so slightly so she could examine his profile: the patrician silver hair tied back in an old-fashioned queue, the heavy eyebrows that made him look perpetually serious, the lines—some deep, some fine as a feather—that defined his face. He watched the drive ahead of them, his mouth arranged in a facsimile of a smile.

This was a man who was unhappy—but didn't want to admit it.

Or didn't know how.

Martha resisted the urge to touch her fingers to his wrist. "Then we two shall fill up Northfield Hall until the younger and more interesting come along."

Lord Preston looked from the horse to her with a quirk of his eyebrow. "Younger they may be, Mrs. Bellamy, but I can hardly think they would be more interesting."

This time, he sounded sincere—and Martha was surprised to notice her heart flutter at the compliment.

Chapter Two

I F Mrs. Bellamy were a lady of the realm, Martin would have known how to introduce her to Northfield Hall. He would have discreetly sent a message ahead of time so that the household servants could assemble in the front hall to greet their guest; he would have whisked Mrs. Bellamy into the garden drawing room for refreshments after her travel; when he gave her a tour of the house, he would have emphasized the architectural elements that great ladies appreciated.

But Mrs. Bellamy was not a lady of the realm, nor was she one of those rector's wives who pretended to be one. She was more like the people who sought labor and refuge at Northfield Hall. In fact, he supposed she now *was* one of those people, since Northfield Hall would be her haven until someone in her family remembered they had a duty to her. Except Martin was not going to ask a poor widow to work for her supper, which meant she was his guest. A guest who would not care about the rococo furniture in the drawing room.

As the gig pulled into the carriage sweep, he shook off his ruminations. He was, as usual, spending too much time thinking and not enough time doing. One of the stable boys rushed over to help with the horse while Jacques, the head footman, descended the Italian marble stairs to assist Mrs. Bellamy to the ground. He greeted her with a familiarity no lady of good breeding would have tolerated:

"It is good to see you, Mrs. Bellamy!"

Martin corrected himself: his daughters would tolerate such a greeting. But then, they had been raised here, and he had never thought it important to impress upon them the finer distinctions of behavior because he had assumed it came naturally as one moved through the world.

He couldn't quite remember how his late wife, Lolly, would have responded, had Jacques expressed such innocent delight at her arrival.

In any case, it was time to move on. He led Mrs. Bellamy up the marble stairs and into the entryway, hoping that the housekeeper Mrs. Chow would magically materialize to smooth over the transaction. Unfortunately, he did not keep the kind of household in which the servants anticipated his every need, and so he and Mrs. Bellamy stood alone in the entrance hall as Jacques unloaded the gig.

"Have you had a tour of the house?" Martin asked, suddenly unable to recall if she had ever visited before. She must have. She was a key part of the Thatcham community, and Martin made a point of keeping relations with Thatcham as warm as possible.

"No, I've only been on the grounds before." Her voice came out a little squeaky, and she cleared her throat. Her eyes were on the walls, which were dark paneled wood adorned with oil paintings the family had collected over the years.

"Ah, then, I'm glad to remedy that before you leave these parts for your family in London." Martin decided to pretend she was a great lady and beckoned her onward to the drawing room at the back of the house. "In comparison to the country houses of my colleagues, the Hall is nothing to speak of, but I am rather fond of it. My great-grandfather rebuilt it after a terrible fire in 1682, so this wing that we are in now is new, so to speak. More windows, better fireplaces, all that comes from modern construction."

Mrs. Bellamy nodded. "From the aftermath of tragedy often springs something new and wonderful."

The trite words felt meaningful from her, for she did not smile to soften them or look his way to see if they landed. She merely said them, as if they were for her and her alone. As if they were a prayer. Martin wondered what new and wonderful thing she had found after the tragic loss of her son—but he stopped himself from asking.

"Yes. In this case, my favorite is this drawing room." With a bit of trepidation, he handed her down the step at the room's threshold.

The great ladies who toured the estate were never impressed by this room. It was too small, its furniture outdated, its design entirely too unfocused on appealing to the eye.

The middle-class visitors who took day tours of Northfield Hall more often exclaimed, "What a lovely room!" But Martin sensed they viewed the aging yellow silk wallpaper—now half a century old—through a veil of judgment. Even the servants and laborers who worked the estate seemed to have little reverence for it, considering it only another room that needed cleaning.

No one ever saw what Martin did: a room for the family to hold fast to each other. A room too small for them to miss each other's words, too beautiful with its picture windows and prospect of the gardens beyond to leave on a sunny afternoon, too comfortable to contaminate conversation with protocol and polite falsities.

Mrs. Bellamy moved into the room only a few steps before stilling, her head and shoulders the only parts of her body moving as she took it in. Martin watched her eyes rove over the amateur watercolors—by his children and Lolly and even a few of the laborers—to the rococo sofas with patched upholstery and the linen drapes tied back to invite in the afternoon sun. At last, she turned her shoulders to set those hazel irises on him. "I can see why you treasure this room."

It was that very moment that the sun shifted to spotlight her in a gentle beam. The mantle of *widow* melted in the golden light, almost like a witch from a fairy tale transforming into a beautiful maiden. There she stood, a sturdy woman with her chin held high, her hair pinned back in a proud bun, brave enough to face her fate.

If he were touched by a fairy's wand, would he, too, transform into a soul strong enough to face fate alone?

The sun shifted, and Martin was freed from the force of such thoughts. He offered Mrs. Bellamy a seat on the pink settee that had been Lolly's favorite. "As I'm sure you know, we don't drink tea or coffee at Northfield Hall, but may I offer you a tisane of peppermint or chamomile?"

"Thank you," she said, looking again like an uncertain old woman, "I shall take whatever you recommend."

MARTHA HAD SUFFERED THROUGH many a tea-taking in her time as rector's wife—especially back in Tolpuddle, when well-to-do people still invited her to their homes—and so she would suffer through this awkward exchange with Lord Preston. She could not precisely define *why* she felt so awkward, for he made warm conversation and asked questions particular to her, unlike so many obligatory teas where the chatter remained on the topic of the hostess's choice, whether the guest had anything to add or not. Nor did Lord Preston make her uncomfortable in any way: he took the seat diagonally across the low table from her so that she could naturally cast her eyes upon the garden beyond the windows rather than him, if she found looking at him to be too taxing.

Not that his prospect *was* taxing. He was a handsome man for their age. Martha had never looked closely upon him before, but now that she sat across from him, she was all too aware of his face, which was pleasing in every aspect, and especially his lips, which were the perfect proportion.

The perfect proportion for *what*, she couldn't say. She simply knew that, were an artist to take him as the model for their painting, they would be pleased with the thin but firm mouth that met them.

In fact, it was not until the maid—a dark-haired, brown-skinned woman of thirty or so—presented them with a Wedgwood porcelain tea set that Martha realized the awkwardness of the afternoon came from the fact that she and Lord Preston were alone in the drawing room.

Martha wasn't sure she had ever had reason to call on a man *alone* before.

And here, she wasn't even calling on Lord Preston. She was moving in with him!

When the maid had withdrawn, Martha made a point of pouring the tea—or, as he had called it, tisane. It was a brew of mint leaves, and the liquid came out pale gold rather than the dark brown to which she was accustomed. "Perhaps I should have let it steep more," she said as she watched it fill the first cup.

"It would not get any darker," Lord Preston assured her. "Tisanes do not show their strength in color the way the tea plant does."

Somewhere along the way, he had discarded his driving gloves, and his fingers were bare as he took the teacup from her. They were elegant yet sturdy, dwarfing the porcelain as he gripped the saucer in one hand and the delicate handle in the other.

Those fingers did not touch hers at all.

He asked, "Will you miss tea very much? Some of our newcomers experience terrible headaches when they are first deprived of tea or coffee."

"I switched over to Mr. Hunt's powder a few months ago. The cost of tea with the duties is too high." The radical reformer Henry Hunt sold a breakfast powder made of chicory root that avoided the tax on tea—but most important to Martha, it lowered her expenses considerably. Ever since Kenneth had died, her imperative had been to spend as little money as possible.

"Ah. You see why I'm of two minds on those duties. I hate to make life harder for anyone who is already barely scraping by, yet they are also effective in curbing some people's consumption of tea."

Martha knew that Lord Preston had long since dictated that Northfield Hall would not purchase anything imported from abroad, but she was curious to hear why from him directly. "What would be achieved if we stopped drinking tea at a national level?"

Up until now, Lord Preston had been so genial that Martha had thought him perfectly engaged in the conversation. But at the question, he lit from within, as if he had swallowed the summer sun wafting in through the open windows. Leaning forward, he set aside his teacup to enumerate his points with his fingers. "If we were to end our consumption of tea, then we would no longer be in debt to China. If we were to end our consumption of coffee, we would no longer support the plantations worked by African slave labor. If we were to end our consumption of sugar and its byproducts rum and molasses, then the slave plantations in the West Indies would have no reason to exist, and we could emancipate all those people. The East Indies sugar production is no better, by the way, and so we must not substitute our purchases but end them entirely. Same with cotton: whether it is coming from the fields of South Carolina or Bengal, it is coming from forced labor."

Martha knew he could have kept going: the American South also grew rice, indigo, and tobacco with slave labor; from Calcutta came cotton and opium of dubious labor practices; from Portugal's colonies in Brazil came mahogany wood tainted by slave labor.

What she wanted to know was whether Lord Preston really believed that Britain could turn its back on these items, or whether, like Eve, once the apple was bitten, there was no returning to Eden.

She should not ask that question, especially not while taking tea—tisane—in his drawing room as his houseguest. Yet as Lord Preston leaned in, the posture of good manners replaced by enthusiasm for his topic, Martha could not help feeling that he would invite the question.

So she took a chance and asked it: "After all these decades of avoiding imports at Northfield Hall, do you think it has made a difference?"

He nodded once to acknowledge the question and retreated backward in his chair. His eyes lifted to a spot behind Martha—to the portrait of his late wife with her children, which hung above the mantel. "Since my marriage in 1788. Which means we have avoided imports for...thirty-five years. Strange to calculate it; so often, I still feel we are at the very beginning of this project."

Her marriage had been longer: she had been twenty-two on her wedding day, and they had been only a month away from their fortieth anniversary when he died.

Of course, Lord Preston's marriage had ended when Lady Preston succumbed to a wasting disease, sometime before Martha had moved to Thatcham. The lady had been gone for at least ten years, perhaps fifteen, yet the look Lord Preston sent the woman in the picture was one of a husband still in his first years of grief.

Martha wished her heart were loving enough to feel that way about Kenneth.

She returned her thoughts to Lord Preston's great project. "Have you achieved what you hoped to by avoiding the import-export economy?"

"My chief aim was to die with a clean conscience," he replied, "and in that respect, I hope I have been successful. The rest of Britain may have a terrible stain on its soul, but I do think that setting an example here at Northfield Hall has made others consider their purchases. Had you thought about where your cotton came from before you moved to Thatcham?"

She had—but only with regards to its quality. "I haven't stopped purchasing cotton when I need it, however."

He smiled kindly. "Not everyone has the luxury of building their own textile works."

The reply sounded—not rehearsed, but perhaps experienced. He had thirty-five years of people informing him they could not join him in avoiding imports, and therefore he had thirty-five years' worth of replies to repair the conversation so no one would leave with great injury to their dignity. Martha couldn't help wondering what his true response was. In his heart, did he judge her for being small-minded? Did he rage that no one appreciated his ingenious vision? Did he grieve that he had been unable to sway the average Briton to care more for the principle of abolition than for their own purse?

Most likely, she reminded herself, he wrote her off as an old woman with a narrow mind who could never have made much of a change in the world even if she wanted to.

"You mustn't feel you need to keep me company," she said, pouring more mint tisane into her teacup even though she had barely sipped it. "I shall be happy if you treat me as you would a governess or some other servant of the family. In fact, if I may do any work at all, please put me to use. I do not know how to be idle."

Lord Preston blinked, that sunlight disappearing from within him, and Martha realized she had rather abruptly changed the subject. Perhaps she was even being indelicate in assigning herself a role for which he was not hiring.

Let him think her rude. She couldn't bear to pretend for one moment longer she was some great lady whom he must entertain with drawing room debate.

"You are my guest, Mrs. Bellamy."

"Surely there is something I can do to be helpful. Perhaps some mending, or polishing the silver."

"I have a whole household of servants to see to such things. Now that I am the only one living here, I'm afraid none of them have enough to do." He pulled out that kind smile again. "No doubt there will be plenty for you to do when you move to your niece's. Embrace this as your season to rest."

Rest. Martha's least favorite activity. "You haven't any open positions? If I had shown up today as a stranger seeking refuge, you would have nothing to offer me and would turn me out?"

"If you were a stranger seeking refuge, we would put you in the lodging house and find some position for you. But, Mrs. Bellamy, you are not a stranger. You are the esteemed late rector's wife, a woman who has already done your share of work for the community. I have invited you here as my guest, and I would not ask you to work in the kitchen or mind the laborers' children."

She almost argued back—but realized, as her mouth opened, that he might be trying to politely remind her that no one wanted to get too close to her, in case Lucas's ending had been not merely a scandal but also a curse.

Lord Preston said apologetically, "The only position I have open at the moment is that of Mr. Maulvi—the steward."

"No, I wouldn't know the first thing about that," she agreed. Then, buoyed by his kindness, she offered, "Do you already have a secretary? I helped my husband with his correspondence all our life. My lettering is better than his." She corrected herself: "Better than his *was*."

The baron measured her with his heavy gaze. "A secretary position requires some discretion, as I correspond on matters of sensitivity to both Northfield Hall and the nation."

Hope allowed Martha to meet him eye for eye. "A rector's wife must be either the biggest gossip in the village or the best at keeping her mouth shut."

His lips curved upward. Martha realized what it was that made them so attractive: when they moved, so did his face, and when he smiled as he did now, it felt as if he were unveiling a secret emotion, just for her.

"Then perhaps, Mrs. Bellamy, you would be so kind as to assist me with my correspondence while you await word from your family."

"Sir," she replied, "it would be my honor."

CHAPTER THREE

T HE CURIOUS THING ABOUT life was how quickly it could change. The previous morning, as Martin had dressed in the clothes laid out for him by his valet West, he had expected a solitary day in a string of solitary weeks as he waited out Parliament's recess at Northfield Hall.

This morning, he rang for West to help him find a better waistcoat than the one he had been wearing of late. He was not wandering the estate on his own anymore, nor was his socializing limited to a visit to poor Maulvi. He could do Mrs. Bellamy the courtesy of wearing clothes without patches.

They were to convene in his study at nine after breakfasting separately. From all the available apartments—of which there were four on the family floor and three above—Mrs. Bellamy had selected the bedroom two doors down the corridor from his. He had suggested it, since its window offered a lovely view straight down the driveway and it did not burden her with an extra chamber for a lady's maid; yet now, he wished he had left the matter entirely to Mrs. Chow so

26

that he wouldn't know the precise location of Mrs. Bellamy at all times.

He didn't know what was the matter with him. He had hosted guests hundreds of times over the years, and never had he second-guessed their room assignments. Just last year, he had, without any of his daughters present as hostesses, entertained two members of the House of Commons and their wives for nearly three weeks. And while he had certainly worn his good waistcoats, he had not spent the early morning straining to hear signs of life from their bedrooms.

What did it serve him to know if Mrs. Bellamy was yet awake?

Martin supposed it was because there was no strategy behind her visit. As practiced a host as he might be, Martin only ever invited people to stay at Northfield Hall for a purpose—usually one related to politics. Martin had no aims for Mrs. Bellamy's visit other than to do his duty by a woman under his umbrella of responsibility. If yesterday he hadn't known how to treat her, then this morning, he didn't know how to feel about her.

Was she intruding on his peace?

Or was she a welcome distraction from his solitude?

He took a simple breakfast of fresh berries and cream and went to prepare his study for her invasion. The truth was that he had never before had a private secretary. At the time he inherited the role of baron, King George III had managed all of *his* correspondence himself, and Martin had decided to follow that example. But Mrs. Bellamy had looked so bereft at the idea of having no duties at Northfield Hall. The offer of the role of secretary had sprung spontaneously from his lips.

It *would* be a help to have someone managing his correspondence so he could spend that time reading reports and planning his strategy for the next round of battle in London. His coalition had accomplished much this year—reducing the number of crimes eligible for the death penalty and transportation, as well as gaol reforms—but, as always, there was still so much to do. Through his son Nate, Martin knew that the African Institution was preparing to publish a report recommending that slave traders be treated as pirates, and he wanted to gather support for legislation to that end before he returned to London in the winter. Too, he wanted to propose another bill to abolish slavery in the empire entirely. And then there were the Corn Laws, which he attacked every year, and the Irish Insurrection Bills, which kept getting renewed to keep the poor country in terror.

And besides all of that, Martin still had to finalize his will.

He was glad Mrs. Bellamy would be assisting him. Yet it also required him to instruct her on what to do and how to do it.

She would be discreet. But she had helped Mr. Bellamy with parish matters. How would she react to the many letters Martin received from the needy and poor and desperate, asking for help he could not give? How would she handle the reports coming in from around the empire recording the terrible conditions of slave plantations and Indian factories?

Martin would limit her to his social correspondence, if he could. Yet he did not write witty letters to grand dames nor engage in prolonged personal exchanges with friends. If he wrote to someone—if someone wrote to him—it had a purpose, and that purpose most likely was more complex than the dilemmas Mr. Bellamy had ever faced.

Martin reminded himself that he was no doubt ruminating so much that everything seemed harder than it was. He would begin by asking her to sort his papers. Ordinarily, his study was relatively orderly, but he had only returned from London the week prior, and he had brought a crate of records which he had so far left untouched on the secretary's desk. It was a simple task that would help both him and Mrs. Bellamy get accustomed to her new role.

She presented herself precisely as the clock in the hall chimed nine. She wore a different set of widow's weeds, and Martin realized that what she had worn the previous day had been a traveling costume. This gown was better suited to summertime—in fact, he suspected it had been recently dyed black from some charming color like sky blue or grassy green, either of which would suit Mrs. Bellamy well. Even black, its cut flattered her curves, its modest neckline highlighting the sweet plumpness of her cheeks.

Feeling awkward, he asked, "Was your breakfast satisfactory?"

"It was delicious, thank you." She hovered on the threshold from the main hall, and Martin realized he hadn't invited her to enter.

In his mind, they were already familiar enough that she need not stand on such ceremony. He waved her in. "This is your desk." It was not as grand as his, which stood in the light of the great bay window catching the morning sun. Her desk was half as wide, with a wooden surface long since scratched by letter openers and pen knives. Martin withdrew the top drawer to display the writing utensils. "If you run out of ink, which you shouldn't anytime soon, Mrs. Chow has it made monthly and can retrieve it from the storeroom for you."

She ran her fingers over the row of pens. They were cherry wood with pale inlaid whirligigs beneath a shining lacquer. A gift from his daughter Ellen when she had first mastered woodworking. She now made him a new set of pens every year for Christmas; the latest featured silhouettes of each of her children.

Mrs. Bellamy's hands were rough and sturdy, evidence of a life without many servants. Yet as they brushed against those pens, they looked gentle. Tender. Caring.

Martin stepped away from the desk. "I have fallen behind on reading the mail since I returned last week. You may begin with that. I should like to see the letters from my family or regarding matters of Parliament. Everything else, set aside. We can review them later this afternoon so you can learn my various standard replies."

"Very well," Mrs. Bellamy said in that handsome voice of hers.

"I'll be right here—" Martin gestured to his desk, only three feet away "—if you have any questions. Which I expect you shall, so please do not be shy in asking them."

She nodded. Once he sat down, she pulled out the heavy desk chair—old wood upholstered in leather—and set a pair of reading glasses on her nose. Martin could see only her profile, yet he had to stop himself from staring: the spectacles made her look at once a decade older and a hundred times more interesting, as if magnifying those hazel eyes illuminated a dozen mysteries for him to solve.

A strange thought to have. To brush it away, Martin picked up a letter from his daughter Sophia. She wanted money, as she often did, and he would have to decide whether to indulge her or remind her she had chosen to live as an accoucheur's wife and now must live within her means.

He hated each time he had to make that decision. He asked Mrs. Bellamy, "How would you compare Thatcham to your previous situation? You were somewhere near the southern coast, I believe."

"Tolpuddle."

Martin was not familiar with the town. He waited, running his eyes over Sophia's letter, until Mrs. Bellamy elaborated:

"We had a living ten miles or so from where I grew up. I used to see my sister nearly every week. It was a good living, too. Not grand, but we brought in enough through the tithes that I could keep a proper household. I even hosted a duchess for tea once."

The words were nice, yet Martin heard a restraint in her voice, as if she used each sentence to plug a dam that was about to burst. He gave her an opportunity to change the subject: "I regret that my family never came to tea at the rectory. I am afraid I often neglect polite company."

"Mrs. Caroline Chow has called several times since her marriage," Mrs. Bellamy said, turning ever so slightly so that her hazel gaze could reach him.

Of course Caroline had visited. She was a Thatcham villager now.

Mrs. Bellamy turned back to the stack of letters. "I loved my life at Tolpuddle. But it came to an end, as all things must, and Thatcham has been good to me. All things considered, people have been very kind."

All things considered referencing her son. Her only child, as far as Martin knew. The son had, at the age of twenty-two, eloped with an earl's daughter; when, within the year, she died of fever because he could afford neither a physician nor medicine, he had shot himself in the head.

It was a story Martin had first read in the newspapers. Later, when the archbishop asked Martin to appoint the vacant Thatcham living to Mr. Bellamy, he had heard it in a hushed explanation of why the grieving parents needed somewhere new to live. Then, when they had arrived, everyone between London and Thatcham had wanted to inform him of exactly what kind of family he had just appointed to be the spiritual stewards of the village.

And when Caroline had first run off with Eddie Chow—oh, how the story had loomed in Martin's heart.

He would not burden Mrs. Bellamy by asking her version of the events. Instead, he said, "You have been very good to Thatcham. Although I am not a regular attendee of Sunday services, I have always heard how good you are to the people of the parish."

"They do not need much compared to Tolpuddle, and that's because of everything you have done at Northfield Hall."

It was true that, with so many people living on his estate and those who lived in Thatcham kept in steady business because of

Northfield, the poor rolls of the parish were all but empty. Martin looked back at his letter. "Enough congratulating each other, then. If we want to keep things going well, we've got to maintain our work."

Mrs. Bellamy—he discovered when he shot a glance her way, to ensure that she didn't take his words as an admonition—smiled to herself in reply.

They worked together companionably for an hour or so, with only a few exchanges as Mrs. Bellamy asked about this letter or that. Martin had started a reply to Sophia—granting her ten of the twenty pounds she requested for traveling to Northfield Hall that Christmas, since after all, she was only coming from London and could make the trip on five pounds—when Mrs. Bellamy asked, "Would you like me to put this letter from your solicitor in the stack of correspondence about your family?"

She held the letter carefully in her two sturdy hands. It was folded open, its seal hanging downward towards the desktop, indicating that she had read it.

His solicitor could have been writing about any number of things. However, their main project at the moment was to decide how Martin should distribute his savings at the time of his death. Which meant Mrs. Bellamy had most likely just read a very sensitive letter answering his questions about who could legally receive the money.

Instinctively, Martin reached out for it. "I'll take it now."

She rose to cross the three feet and place it in his hands. His embarrassment surging, he added:

"I am of course going to do right by my children. The challenge is to predict how much they shall need the money compared to all the investments that Northfield Hall requires."

"Of course." Mrs. Bellamy surrendered the letter.

"There is the question of principle, as well, by which I mean ethics and not fiscal principal." Martin found he could not stop explaining himself. "As a father, I want to ensure my children and their families are provided with all possible resources to succeed. Yet a founding idea of Northfield is that our profits should be shared amongst everyone who lives and works here. Should that not extend to the distribution of my wealth after I die? And what about the property? Legally, I cannot will away anything that is entailed to the title, but the surrounding acres...should I leave that in a trust to the people of Northfield?"

He only stopped because if he were to continue with the other questions swirling in his head, he might no longer be able to breathe.

Mrs. Bellamy reached across the desk and placed her well-worn palm over his hand. Warm skin. Soft eyes. "No parent ever knows what is best. We only do what we can."

Martin's fingers curled around Mrs. Bellamy's. "I'm sorry that we did not reform for burials of *felo de se* until this year. It must be very hard not having a grave to visit."

She blinked, and for the first time, Martin saw grief steal across her face. He was sorry to be the cause of it. He did not want to be one of those people who opened old wounds for their own benefit.

But before he could apologize, Mrs. Bellamy said, "Thank you," and she remained there, bent across the desk to hold his hand, for a moment longer.

IT WAS AS IF the moment she had entered his study, Martha had crossed the threshold into a fairy realm, one that looked the same as her known world yet contained some other woman—a woman who could cling to the baron's hand as the emotions she had buried for so many years rose like a groundwater flood.

A moment like this would ordinarily have frozen Martha into silence; she should excuse herself from the room to recover from the embarrassment of her familiarity with Lord Preston. She should flee before she did something worse, like cry.

The most she could bring herself to do was release his hand—though her fingers immediately felt bereft, in the same way her arms used to long for Lucas the moment she handed her baby to someone else.

"Thank you," she said again, trying to gather herself.

"I hate to cause you pain all over again by bringing it up."

Martha heard herself laugh—a short bark for which Kenneth would have scolded her if he were alive to hear it. "It causes me pain whether you remind me of it or not, sir."

He leaned forward, his elbows propped on the desktop, chin stacked on his steepled fingers. His eyes were dark and warm and kind. "That is the way of grief, isn't it."

"Grief, yes." She should agree and let it be. It was time to retreat to her desk. Yet Martha found herself, in this fairy realm, remaining there with Lord Preston. "Shame, too. Dismay. Guilt. I—" But she didn't know where her sentence was going. All those words she had been holding in remained trapped, lost somewhere in their exile.

Lord Preston watched her without a reply of his own.

Martha confessed: "I wonder if having a grave to visit would make it easier. I've been visiting Kenneth's every day so that I could see if it helps with the grief. I pretend Lucas is there under that marker with his father. But he's not, and I can't forget that he is not. The truth is that I don't know where he is. What kind of mother doesn't know where her child is?"

Lord Preston nodded, and his silence was what allowed her to keep going:

"I know he is buried at a crossroads near Bath, but I don't know which. I know that they drove a stake through his heart before they buried him. I know all of that is supposed to punish him, but I don't see how. God is already punishing him. It only punishes *me*." Here came a—not a sob, not a gasp, but a breath that tore through her like a tornado. Martha gripped Lord Preston's desk to recover. Her eyes were burning and hot, and when she wiped at them, she discovered tears had been gathering on her lashes.

Reaching across the desk, Lord Preston circled her wrist with his fingers as a bulwark.

"Maybe it's right that I'm punished. Maybe that is the whole design. After all, what kind of mother raises a son who runs off with an earl's daughter? Where was his common sense? Where was his idea of right and wrong? Aren't his sins my sins, too?"

Lord Preston's fingers tightened around the bare skin of her wrist, almost as if he were checking her pulse. His dark eyes broke away from watching her as he said, "What kind of father raises a daughter who spurns her family to marry a glazier?"

Strange—Kenneth had failed Lucas just as much as Martha had, yet this moment with Lord Preston was the first time that her guilt no longer felt like hers alone. She *was* guilty, but so was the mighty Lord Preston, and that made it more bearable.

His fingers withdrew from her wrist. Still looking down, he said, "No doubt you resent the comparison. Not only is Caroline alive, but she and I are on speaking terms."

"I don't resent you." Martha wanted to take his hand again, but she didn't have the courage. Somehow, the fairy dust was wearing off, and soon she would need to return to the desk with the correspondence and continue with life as if Lucas had never lived and erred and died. In these last moments, she added, "I commiserate with you, and I thank you for that."

Lord Preston looked up at her again at last, and he smiled the kind of smile only fellow warriors could share.

Perhaps she had once shared that kind of smile with Kenneth, but Martha didn't remember it. This felt new—special—freeing—intoxicating.

Martha retreated to her desk. She spent the rest of the morning sorting Lord Preston's mail, and they didn't have any further conversation. Yet the feeling remained in the air, a secret between just the two of them, and for the first time in years, Martha found herself wishing time would slow.

CHAPTER FOUR

THE NEXT FINE DAY, Martin ordered the gig to be prepared for a ride around the estate after breakfast. He had taken one tour of Northfield upon his return from London, but it had been cursory, his object to greet people rather than to discover the problems that needed his attention. Now he owed the property a day of tending to its hedges that needed training, fields that needed draining, and buildings that needed painting.

He had debated mentioning the idea to Mrs. Bellamy at supper the night before—which they had taken at one of the small tables in his study in the long light of the summer evening, while discussing inconsequential matters like the art that hung on his walls. They had by now spent several days together, and Martin found himself deliberately keeping the conversation away from anything that might feel meaningful.

He thought too much about that moment when they had clasped hands across his desk. He didn't want to risk repeating it.

And so the night before he had not invited her to tour North-field with him. Yet, as he heard the maid clearing away Mrs. Bellamy's breakfast tray down the corridor, he found himself picturing what she would do in his absence. Would she borrow a book from his shelves? (She had expressed interest in reading his collection of works by Thomas Paine—"Only so that I may understand why they upset everyone.") Would she catch up on her own correspondence, instead of spending her energy on his? Would she know she could open the garden drawing room windows to let in the breeze?

He remembered her agitation on their first afternoon together when he had suggested she rest. It was not simply the industriousness of a woman used to hard work. If he had learned anything from these few days together, it was that being idle exposed Mrs. Bellamy to the dangers of her own heart.

Martin hated to leave anyone in danger. And besides, as he anticipated the hard bench of the gig, he decided he did not care to spend the whole day apart from his new friend.

He rapped on her bedroom door before he could second-guess himself. In the brief moment before she answered, he realized his awkward position: What if she wore only a dressing gown?

What kind of dressing gown would Mrs. Bellamy own, any-how? He pictured something well-worn, let out over the years, perhaps with patches at the elbows; it might even be a robe remaining from before her son died, a relic from that happy part of her life that she was not yet ready to release.

The door opened. Mrs. Bellamy looked up at him in her black cotton summer dress. She was missing only two parts of her outfit: the cap that ordinarily covered her silver hair, and shoes. Without the black cap, her face looked fresher, the creases around her eyes and mouth less pronounced, and her cheeks pinker. Martin looked down to discover her feet peeking out from beneath the hem of her dress in nothing but stockings—those were dyed black, grief seizing even her ankles.

He cleared his throat. "I am touring the estate today. If you would like to accompany me, I could use your assistance making note of necessary repairs."

Her cheeks flushed pink. "I would not be in your way?"

"You would be of great help. However, it will not be as comfortable as a day in the house. If you should like to remain behind and stay cool, I would understand."

"No, I'll join you." She lingered for a moment after saying it, making no move either to shut the door or collect her shoes. Martin found himself pinned in place, too. There was something about moving that would break a spell, and the spell was a good enchantment, the kind that made him feel like smiling.

Friendship. After all, he had always wanted Maulvi to accompany him on tours of the property. Mrs. Bellamy was his new trusted helper.

Nothing more.

Martin cleared his throat. "I'll go check on the gig. When you're ready, meet me in the stable yard."

It was a hot day for that summer, which had so far been remarkably cool. Martin donned a straw hat to keep the sun off his face, yet by the time Mrs. Bellamy joined him in the stables, he had to wipe sweat from his brow. She had changed into her traveling costume—no doubt to keep dust from ruining her day gown—and wore her reading glasses on a leather string like a necklace. He let the groom help her into the gig while he hoisted himself in on the opposite side.

When they had ridden together from Thatcham, Mrs. Bellamy had held herself stiff as a board, careful not to let even her skirts touch him. This time, as Martin negotiated the horse onto the path leading out of the stable yard, she relaxed against the backboard and her dark worsted skirt fanned against the ankles of his sturdy leather boots.

"I have heard Farmer Griffin worry about his wheat this year on account of how cold the weather has been," Mrs. Bellamy said. "Are you concerned about the crops here at Northfield?"

"One must always be concerned about the crops." The agricultural societies had published several tracts on the subject of the cool weather; everyone remembered the bad harvest of 1816, which had led to starvation throughout the country, which had led to civil unrest.

Maulvi had always cautioned that Northfield should assume a bad year would follow a good one, and so they must lay in stores to suffer through failed crops. Still, Martin couldn't help but worry, especially as the rooms at Northfield Hall continued to fill. He added to Mrs. Bellamy, "Our crops this year so far are a little less robust than usual, but we have every hope of a good harvest."

He drove the gig across the property to the trade village, where a collection of stone buildings housed Northfield's smithies, masonry, carpentry workshop, and other necessary craft shops. Hopping down from the gig—less of a hop, really, more of a creaking leap at which his knees protested—he hitched the horse to the post beside the well in the center of the village. Then Martin helped Mrs. Bellamy from the gig. Palms on either side of her soft waist. Her hands braced on his shoulders. A whiff of her perfume as her face drew close to his.

From across the common, Mr. Beauchamp hailed him. "Lord Preston!"

Martin summoned patience before turning towards the man. He already knew what this would be about, and he still didn't have an answer to the question.

"May we offer you a refreshment? Tisane, or perhaps my wife's chilled apple cider for this fine morning?"

Beauchamp and his wife had been at Northfield almost as long as the Chow family, having fled the French regime as Napoleon seized power. They served as Northfield Hall's tallow makers, keeping the estate in fresh supply of candles and soap.

Unfortunately, that meant their workshop was the smelliest of the trade village. Martin hated to subject Martha to the experience, especially when he already knew how the conversation would go.

"Thank you, Beauchamp, however, I am afraid we haven't the time this morning. Have you met Mrs. Bellamy? She is the widow of the late rector of Thatcham and is helping me in Mr. Maulvi's absence."

Beauchamp nodded politely. Martin supposed that, since the Beauchamps were Catholic, they had never had much cause to cross paths with the Bellamys.

"As to the question of the cottages, I have not yet found a solution, but I am hopeful that after a closer review of the estate today, I may have some clever ideas," Martin said.

"Thank you, my lord." Beauchamp bowed a little, in a way that was embarrassing to both him and Martin. "My youngest and his bride are very eager. I hope to have good news for them soon."

"Indeed."

Martin regretted feeling so impatient with the man. It was only natural that Beauchamp should expect his children to all be able to remain at Northfield and that each child should, with their own family, expand into a cottage of their own. Yet the Beauchamps had trained all their sons for tallow making when the estate only needed the one workshop, and there were no more cottages available.

If the question was how Martin could find a way to keep all the Beauchamp children at Northfield, then he knew there was a creative solution somewhere.

However, he was all too aware that the question was larger than the Beauchamps. He needed an answer he could offer everyone, not just Mr. Beauchamp, and he did not yet have one.

Mrs. Bellamy did not ask any questions as Martin led her across the courtyard to the carpentry workshop. Still, he felt her observant eyes on him, and he feared what conclusions she might be drawing from his curt exchange with Mr. Beauchamp.

"On days like this, I miss my daughter Ellen particularly," he said. "She is a trained carpenter herself, you know, and would be thrilled to assist me on this errand. I find there is no better time spent with a person than when observing them engaged in their passions."

Mrs. Bellamy smiled. "I have heard many stories of the countess. I confess, I have wondered why you permitted her to learn the trade."

In the wake of Caroline's betrayal, Martin had wondered that himself. Why had he and Lolly not ensured their children understood the behavior expected of their class? They had wanted each child to think critically and independently about the world around them, but why had they not insisted on the girls learning to be ladies, too?

Martin supposed that he hadn't realized how much of that needed to be taught. And when Ellen would have been escorted to assembly halls for practice balls or taken to London for a Season, Lolly had been ill, then dying, then dead.

"I have a terrific speech to answer that question to anyone in London," Martin confessed to Mrs. Bellamy, "but the truth is that I was distracted by my wife's illness. I would have permitted just about anything that kept my children occupied and happy."

They were at the door to the carpentry workshop, but he hesitated to knock on it, glancing instead at the woman at his side to see her reaction. Her smile was gone, replaced with a look that was becoming familiar to him. One of fellow feeling. One of compassion.

He worried he had made that confession just to earn that look from her again.

At last, he knocked on the door and was answered, as expected, by Spencer Chow. Spencer was the second eldest of the Chow boys and the only one who remained at Northfield—unless one counted Eddie in Thatcham, which Martin did not. He bowed at the neck to greet them.

"I wonder if you could spare some time for me this morning to examine the women's dormitories," Martin said.

"Yes, sir." Removing his apron and work gloves, Spencer rearranged some tools and donned his coat before joining them at the gig.

Assuming they hadn't met, Martin conducted the introductions: "This is Mrs. Bellamy, widow of the late rector. Spencer Chow, our head carpenter."

Mrs. Bellamy smiled politely. "We have met a few times at Mrs. Caroline Chow's fetes."

Caroline hosted fetes? As far as Martin knew, she and Eddie lived in a two-room house leased from one of the Thatcham farmers. Where could she play hostess? And when?

Perhaps they had all happened while Martin was in London, which was why no one had seen fit to inform him of them.

Spencer, as usual, found the least amount of words to make a reply and then hoisted himself onto the back of the gig. Mrs. Bellamy hiked up her skirt to climb up to the bench.

Martin could let her do it herself. With either hand gripping the gig and her foot already firmly planted on a spoke, she seemed more than capable of managing it. But her skirt fell backward, revealing a stockinged ankle above her half-boots, and Martin had a premonition of her leg twisting in the wheel.

"Permit me," he begged, and he lifted her by the waist.

Their eyes met as she settled on the bench. Martin couldn't help but notice her lashes flutter like a lady's fan at a ball.

If they were younger—if she were not a somber widow—he might assume she was flirting with him.

But he did not want that. And she was most certainly not making such an overture, not when she was in the throes of grief. Martin was being silly, like a young buck in his first Season.

He hiked himself onto the bench and drove the gig towards the dormitory.

MARTHA SUPPOSED EVERY WOMAN who found herself in the path of Lord Martin Preston ended up dazzled by him. He was too handsome, too intelligent, too kind not to incite excitement in the hearts of those around him.

No doubt he had a dozen noble ladies courting him every Season in London.

Even more likely, he had a mistress tucked away in some respectable neighborhood, paid a generous sum and treated like a wife in every way except sacred matrimony.

Martha would not judge him for it. The man was a baron: he couldn't marry just anyone that he fell in love with, especially not when he had to keep a sterling reputation for his coalition in Parliament. Yet he was such a feeling man. He deserved the love of a good woman—or, Martha supposed, of a woman who loved him back, since a mistress who accepted such terms could hardly be a *good* woman.

In any case, she was quite sure her breathless excitement each time they were within reach of each other was exclusively on her part. It did not dull Martha's feelings that he would not be dazzled in return by her, an old woman. The sensation of bubbling like champagne because he was near, the habit of collecting observations throughout her day and imagining how he might respond, the primping in front of her looking glass to make sure her hair was just right—Martha was enjoying it all. She hadn't been consumed by such frivolity since Lucas died, and therefore had assumed it was a part of her life she would never get back. She hadn't even *wanted* it, especially not with Kenneth constantly reminding her she had to behave properly or else bring the scorn of Thatcham down upon them.

Who could have guessed that at sixty-two, she would be riding in a gig next to a gentleman hoping that their arms might bump together?

It was enough to make her feel alive again.

The ride from the trade village to the women's dormitory did not take long—and provided no fateful tilts that would have slid her down the bench into Lord Preston's lap. Which was just as well, since Mr. Spencer Chow was there to observe her girlish foolishness. Still, Martha waited as primly as a fine lady for Lord Preston to help her down from the gig. When his hands framed her waist, she allowed herself to press as close to his shoulders as she needed.

Their cheeks almost kissed.

And then the ground was under her feet and she had to let go. Still, joy bubbled through her, and Martha curled her fingers to try to keep the memory of his body inside them.

She shifted her attention to the task at hand: the dormitory. It was a brick building several hundred feet long and four stories high. Its façade was redder than that of Northfield Hall, its shingle roof newer. For a single woman, it must be a fine place to live.

"Would you be so kind as to go in and inquire whether there is anyone about who would be disturbed by Spencer and me entering?" Lord Preston asked her.

Part of her feelings for him were simply that he made her feel useful. Martha tried not to preen as she answered, "Certainly."

Inside, the building smelled of lumber and coal fire. The ground floor featured a staircase where she entered, a long hallway of rooms, and another staircase on the other end. Martha knocked on a door or two and, getting no reply, called out, "Is there anyone about?"

For good measure, she climbed up to each floor and called out the same, never getting a reply. As she did, she noted the whitewashed walls, the well-tended fireplaces, the clean smell of the place. It had none of the marks of dilapidation that she had noted around the great house—whose wallpapers were stained and scarred, whose carpets were beginning to show patches, and whose windows seemed to jam more often than they opened. To Martha's eye, the grounds of Northfield Hall received much better care than the house in which the Preston family lived.

A little breathless from the exertion of climbing four flights of stairs, Martha returned to where Lord Preston and Mr. Chow awaited her. "It seems everyone is at work."

"Thank you." Lord Preston beckoned Mr. Chow inside. His voice adopting the low, melodious tone he used when explaining, he said, "We have only one vacant room at the moment, and in the last year, we have had at least three new women presenting themselves every month. While single men tend to stay at Northfield Hall for six months or a year as they bide a bad season, the women who come tend to stay, and I never want to turn anyone away or ask them to leave. With a little ingenuity, Spencer, do you think we shall be able to add rooms to the existing floorplan?"

Mr. Chow replied with a thoughtful grunt and tilted his head at the corridor.

Together, the three of them walked the length of the building. Lord Preston and Mr. Chow discussed various ideas: Could a room fit underneath the stairwell? Could the larger rooms be split in two and still provide a reasonable living space? Could one of the staircases be removed entirely and replaced with an extra set of rooms?

Martha trailed a few steps behind them at all times, reading glasses on as she jotted down their ideas in the traveling notebook she had brought along. She also wrote down the things Lord Preston seemed to take for granted: that each room should have a window, so that every individual had access to daylight; that the fireplaces must remain, so that the building would not get too cold in the winter; that no two people must be required to share a room, even if it could fit two ticks, because each laborer deserved some small space of their own with a door they could shut.

They were dignified requirements. They were radical requirements. Hearing him list them as if they were as basic as that every person should eat a meal each day filled Martha with admiration. This was why everyone in Britain knew his name—and why his correspondence was full of strangers asking him for advice, for help, for money. Lord Preston saw the world differently than the rest of their leaders did, and he made a person want to join him in that vision.

Unfortunately, there was no clear solution for adding rooms to the dormitory. When they had exhausted their inspection of the inside, Spencer led them out to examine the strip of land beside the building, onto which they could add a second wing or a separate building entirely. Yet to expand, either a farm field must be cleared or a narrow, boggy patch of land must be tamed.

"Could be a better place to build," Spencer offered as they returned to the gig.

"Yes," Lord Preston agreed with a sigh, "there must be."

The carpenter walked himself back to the trade village while Martha and Lord Preston moved on to review the textile works. These, too, were in better condition than the great house, yet the barn roof required repair and its walls needed repainting. And Mrs. Shayler, the supervisor of the looms, warned, "We'll have less surplus to sell to London this year, my lord, since we've got that many more people to clothe here on the estate."

Lord Preston didn't sigh this time, but Martha noticed his lips compress as he accepted the news with a nod.

"You are no doubt noticing the pattern, Mrs. Bellamy," he said as they set off in the gig back towards the great house. "There isn't enough of anything this year. Not enough crops, not enough space, not enough linens..."

"Quite enough people, I should say." Martha meant it to cheer him up, but she feared it sounded like a reprimand. "You are to be commended for welcoming so many of us in our darkest hours."

He relaxed against the back of the bench. "I hope not everyone is in their darkest hour. Some people present themselves simply because they have heard Northfield is the very best place to be."

"Then I hope they are worthy of your generosity."

His lips—those handsome lips that she couldn't stop watching!—compressed again. "I struggle with that philosophy."

"Which philosophy?"

"That I am being generous. It often feels like generosity, and I am always glad to hear the compliment. However, when I stop to examine it, I am not sure it qualifies as generosity to share the land with those who work it. Is that not fairness? Is that not how we are intended to behave?"

Martha could see this was not simply a debate to keep his mind active but a question that plagued him. She replied as best she could: "Do you not believe in the natural order of the world and that we are intended to care for each other through the great chain, beginning with God and going all the way down to the ants in the anthill?"

The gig rolled past the pond, whose water glittered with a greenish hue in the noontime sun, as Lord Preston selected the words for his reply. "Forgive me if I offend you, but I do not believe it is part of the divine plan, if there is such a thing. I think that because it is how our society behaves, it is an order to which we must adhere or else risk great chaos, but I do not think it is the correct moral code."

Martha shouldn't have been surprised that the radical Lord Preston would espouse radical ideas. If printed, such a sentiment could get him locked in prison for blasphemy. Still, even with her heart racing at the joy of being near him, she found her hands folding primly in her lap, as if that would protect her from his words.

"Caroline accused me of being unwilling to break that great chain when I forbade her to marry Eddie," Lord Preston continued, his voice a little raw. "And to a certain degree, she is right. I am unwilling to throw off the great chain. I am still a baron; I have not renounced the system of aristocracy and thrown in my lot with the Americans. I see the humanity in every person who lives here at Northfield, but I do not insist we all live equally. When my daughter—well, I thought it was dangerous for her to marry Eddie, for both their sakes. But none of that means it is *right*. It is simply the way things are at this moment in time, in this particular place. After all, the plantation owners argue that they care for their slaves as part of the great chain—and I repudiate that every chance I get."

Radical indeed—Martha had never heard the idea of renouncing aristocracy, and certainly not from an aristocrat himself.

"If I spend my fortune on purchasing land to build new cottages and dormitories and increase our production, is that generosity? How can I even call it my money, when it is all earned by the labor that hundreds of people do collectively? Would you call a steward generous for fulfilling his responsibility?" Before she had a chance to answer, he continued: "Yet if I invest in Northfield so it can keep growing as it wants to do, then I will have no money left for my family. Am I not a father first? Must I not guard the family's fortune so that we do not end up in need of the very sanctuary that Northfield Hall provides?"

No—Martha didn't believe that anyone could sit beside Lord Preston for three days, as she had, and not be enchanted with him. Who else was so careful and selfless and honest and brave?

He offered her a self-deprecating smile. "I am sorry to burden you with these ruminations. I am often guilty of thinking too thoroughly about things, but on this matter, I am afraid I still have much contemplating to do."

Martha gave in to the urge she had resisted all morning and threaded her hand through the crook of his elbow. "Yours is not an easy path, sir. It is no burden at all to walk it with you for a little while."

His smile blossomed, and Martha dared imagine it was because his heart, too, was leaping at her touch.

Chapter Five

On Sunday, Caroline came for a midday dinner. Martin had gone over the menu with Mrs. Chow on Friday and again Saturday afternoon to make sure they were serving Caroline's favorites. Mrs. Chow humored him, as she always did. They had known each other since she and her husband showed up in Martin's garden, begging for help after being turned out by his neighbor on account of her expecting a baby. That had been his impetus for turning Northfield Hall into an estate that welcomed anyone who needed safe haven. Since then, Mrs. Chow had been Lolly's maid, nurse to his children, and for the last couple of decades, housekeeper.

Now she was Caroline's mother-in-law, too. Which meant that, when Caroline and Eddie arrived at noontime in their rickety gig, Martin went out of his way to invite Mrs. Chow and her husband to join them at the table. "Please, you are family," he insisted with all the grace he would show to the king himself.

"No, thank you, we couldn't," Mrs. Chow replied, as she always did.

"Please, Mama Chow," Caroline said, using the new name she had invented for the woman she had known since birth. "Eddie and I should like to spend time with you and Father Chow, too."

"Come visit us after, then. We are minding the little ones today."

"Oh, but bring them along! What family is not entertained by its littlest members?" Clapping her hands, Caroline looked at Martin with equal parts appeal and accusation. "You would welcome my nephew and niece at the table, wouldn't you, Papa?"

The children—Spencer's offspring—were hardly old enough for company, but Martin dutifully and sincerely answered, "Of course. Please, Mrs. Chow, do join us."

But she shook her head. "Perhaps another time. Today—" she looked pointedly at Mrs. Bellamy "—you have a guest."

Martin, of course, had not forgotten Mrs. Bellamy, not even for an instant. She stood in a little corner of the foyer as if she thought that would make her invisible, a friendly expression pasted to her lips in case anyone should look over. Martin wondered what she thought of the exchange. Did she see it for the farce it was, one in which everyone except for Caroline already knew the outcome?

Or did she, like Caro, think he was failing to apply himself hard enough to make Mr. and Mrs. Chow feel part of his family?

"We'll see you after the meal," Eddie said, putting one arm around Caro's shoulders and bowing his head to his mother. "Hopefully before little Mary's nap."

It was not that Martin did not like having Mr. and Mrs. Chow at the family table. He had hosted them in London when Eddie had finished his apprenticeship in the same dining room where he lobbied William Wilberforce! But everyone had their routines at Northfield Hall. Surely the Chows would feel as strange sitting in the dining room as Martin would if he decided to sup in their cottage.

He was not saying it was *right*, as Caroline seemed to think, only that it was *comfortable*, and they did not need to fight nature on this particular subject.

The matter settled, they moved into the dining room. They all sat at one end, Martin at the head of the table with Caroline and Eddie on his right and Mrs. Bellamy on his left. The weather had once again turned cool, so a fire burned in the hearth and the windows remained shut against the drizzling rain. Despite the size of the room—the table stretched onwards to seat sixteen people, with space for footmen to bustle around serving dish after dish—Martin felt a little suffocated.

He shook off the feeling. How lucky he was that Caroline and Eddie had traveled five miles to spend an afternoon with him. He would make the most of this precious time with his daughter.

"Oh, Mrs. Bellamy," Caro began, "I have a letter for you from Mr. Sebright."

Mrs. Bellamy accepted the letter with that faux-friendly look. "How was service this morning? Have you had a chance to meet Mrs. Sebright?"

"The church was quite full. I imagine everyone was eager to find out what kind of service Mr. Sebright would give. As to Mrs. Sebright, we had a brief conversation about the school, but there is much more to discuss."

Wanting to avoid awkwardness around the fact that neither he nor Caroline regularly attended Sunday services, Martin said, "I have heard from Mrs. Bellamy that you are a most active hostess in Thatcham, Caro. Have you any upcoming fetes planned?"

"This is not London society, Papa. I'm not hosting *fetes*."

Her tone hovered between belligerent and rude.

But he was not the father who could scold her, anymore. He had to be grateful that she was gracing him with her company. Still, his hackles rose—and in defense of Mrs. Bellamy, too.

Mrs. Bellamy said kindly, "Perhaps I used the wrong word, sir, having no experience of London myself. What would you call your spring event, Mrs. Chow? A gathering?"

Caroline had the grace to look a little embarrassed that her vitriol had landed on poor Mrs. Bellamy instead of Martin. "Yes, I suppose so. After all, there was neither dancing nor music. We were congratulating each other on surviving the winter, as well as raising money to send Daniel Cropper to Edinburgh for medical school."

Martin resented her use of "we." Was he not a part of Thatcham, at least enough to be invited to a spring gathering? "I should have been happy to make a contribution."

"You were in London."

He could still have sent money. He would have *happily* sent money, if only she had asked.

"Uncle Maulvi collected a contribution from Northfield," Caroline added, "so do not worry that anyone thinks you have shirked your duty."

As if all that mattered to him was the appearance of benevolence. Or as if all that mattered from the transaction was that the money was exchanged—whether Martin knew about it or not. He swallowed back his objection. "Then I shall thank Uncle Maulvi when next I call on him."

They all seemed to mutually recognize a safe topic. Eddie said, "We stopped in on him this morning, and he was looking well, all things considered."

"Such a kind man," Mrs. Bellamy added. "He and my late husband enjoyed several long discussions about faith and theology, though Mr. Bellamy never expected to find anything in common with a Mohammedan."

Caro smiled. "No doubt that is why he and Papa are so well suited. They both like to debate things to death."

Martin wanted to add something to this turn of conversation. But when he opened his mouth to call Maulvi his best friend, the words died in his throat.

It was too much like eulogizing the man—and Martin still clung to the hope that he would never have to do that.

Clearing his throat—tucking back all the emotion that threatened to emerge—Martin asked Caroline, "And how are you feeling these days?"

She was several months into her first pregnancy, with the baby expected in the winter. "I feel fine, Papa." This time, her tone bordered on fond. "Eddie sees to my every need."

Eddie's hand covered hers as she said it, and they exchanged a small, secret smile. That was one thing Martin had never doubted: Eddie was and had always been devoted to Caroline.

Still, it was strange to imagine his grandchildren growing up as the children of a glazier instead of peers of the realm.

"I have invited Sophia and John to spend the winter here," Martin said, "so that John may be at your disposal as the time nears." John Anderson, who was married to Martin's daughter Sophia, was one of the most coveted accoucheurs in Britain.

"They needn't come on my behalf. Midwife Brimble always did right by Ellen, and I'm sure she'll do right by me."

Martin wondered if Caro would reply so stubbornly if Sophia had been the one to suggest it, not him. "Why not make use of both the midwife and the accoucheur? Surely it cannot hurt to have two experts in the room with you."

"All the women of Thatcham are happy with Midwife Brimble. Why should I require an accoucheur when none of them do?"

Martin knew he should not argue back—but when Caroline got this stubborn, he always seemed to respond by digging in his own heels.

Luckily, Eddie interrupted before Martin could make it worse. "If John is here anyhow, Monkey, it couldn't hurt to have his advice. After all, just remember how the fever took Mrs. Griswick when her baby came in breech..."

"I'm much younger than Mrs. Griswick, and I am perfectly healthy so far. Besides, we can hardly pay John's fee."

This time, Mrs. Bellamy cut in before either Martin or Eddie could make it worse. "It's always different, for every woman and with every baby. No need to worry about it until the time comes, I like to say." Not quite smiling, she said directly to Caro, "I'd trust Midwife Brimble with my life."

Caroline's eyes suddenly shone with tears, surprising Martin. She brushed them away, cleared her throat, and changed the subject. "Is there any news from Benjamin, Papa? Last I heard, you invited him to spend the winter here, too."

When she said it like that, it sounded as if Martin was begging each of his children to come keep him company until Parliament reconvened. "With Uncle Maulvi retired, I should prefer to prepare Benjamin for Northfield Hall than hire a new steward. After all, my life can only last so much longer."

Here, he paused, waiting for Caroline to object that of course he would live forever. She only knocked on the tabletop—superstitiously warding off bad spirits—as she bit into another forkful of mutton.

Martin had no choice but to continue: "I haven't heard back from him yet, however. Perhaps his reply will be to show up in person. Preferably with Lydia and the boys, too."

Caroline nodded. "It takes a long time for a letter to reach Galway, after all."

"What a joy it would be for you to have so many of your children at home," Mrs. Bellamy said. This time, nothing about her comment felt compelled from politeness. Her smile for Martin was as genuine as her happiness for him.

Martin grinned back, even though he felt every emotion other than joy as he tried to wrangle his children back into his orbit. He knew he needn't explain that to Mrs. Bellamy. She understood, without him saying, that these relationships with his children who were no longer children were too complicated, just as he knew that as painful as they were at times, they were far less painful than the tragedy she had endured.

"It would be a joy," he agreed. He turned his smile onto Caroline. "I am grateful that at least one of you has remained nearby so that I need not always beg for visits."

But this, apparently, was the wrong thing to say. Anger flashed through Caro's eyes before she could hide it by looking down at her plate.

Perhaps it was too much of a reminder that he had at first tried to push her away so that she would not end up living in a cottage at Northfield Hall married to Eddie. Martin had long since apologized for that—and Caroline said she forgave him.

But she certainly hadn't forgotten.

"Speaking of letters," she said, "I have been corresponding with Mr. Mudie, who of late organized the Owenite community at Spa Fields. Their aims are much like yours, Papa, of changing our economy to value labor over money. However, instead of the whole community kowtowing to an aristocratic benefactor, they are made up of working-class men and women who share their labor."

Martin had, of course, been closely following the Spa Fields group, who called themselves the Cooperative and Economical Society. He, too, corresponded with Mr. Mudie—as well as Robert Owen himself, the man inspiring labor-based communities as a solution to poverty. But the way Caroline said it—the words she used—made it clear she meant this to start an argument.

An argument Martin should steer clear of, since it would only drive her further from him instead of proving that he was, in fact, worthy of her trust.

But he couldn't help himself.

"Kowtow? I do not believe I have ever asked a single person to *kowtow* to me." It was a singular word, one printed by observers of the Chinese court and not one that Martin considered favorable. It conjured images of blind obedience—of emperors banishing courtiers for not bowing deeply enough.

It was exactly the kind of accusation Caroline *would* levy against him, as if his expectation that she marry someone of her own class had proven that he was in fact the devil incarnate.

"Neither do you tell them not to."

"Did I not just invite Mrs. Chow to dine with us? Find me one other baron who would do so, whether he is related to her by marriage or not."

"Yet she said no because she finds it uncomfortable. After all these years, she still calls you Lord Preston."

"It is my *title*!"

"If you truly do not want people to kowtow, you would do as the Quakers do and instruct us to ignore your title."

"I did not realize that on top of everything else, you now expect me to become a Quaker. I apologize, Caroline, but as I have sworn to uphold the thirty-nine articles of the Church of England, I'm afraid I cannot make that conversion just for you."

"I am asking nothing of you, Papa. I depend upon you for nothing."

And there it was—the ugly truth that always hovered between them. Caroline was happily married to Eddie now, but not because Martin had enabled it. No—she lived in Thatcham and hosted her gatherings and expected a baby because she had been headstrong and her siblings had supported her.

She had never even asked Martin for her dowry.

And because of that, Martin did not dare expect anything from her. He had to hope she would continue to come to Sunday dinners every now and then, and he had to be on his best behavior lest she decide he was not worth introducing her children to. He was the father who was neither disowned nor loved.

What would Lolly think, if she could visit him now?

What *did* Mrs. Bellamy think, trapped at the dinner table as they hurled feral emotions at each other?

Eddie put his hand over Caroline's again, and she let out an angry exhale. "I'm overexcited. I had better lie down for a little."

Martin, too, tried to dismiss his hurt and reply like the father he wanted to be. "The beds are all made upstairs. Rest for as long as you need. You and Eddie can both spend the night, if necessary."

But Caroline, already rising from her chair, shook her head. "I'll go rest at Mr. and Mrs. Chow's. I can sit in their rocker chair and enjoy the children while I recover my spirits."

Martin stood out of good manners. Jacques—who, of course, had heard the whole exchange—waited at the entryway with Caroline's cloak. Eddie bowed his head—kowtowed?—to Martin. "I'm sorry things got unpleasant. We'll see you soon."

And then they were gone, their meals half eaten. Martin looked at Mrs. Bellamy, tried to find some apology or excuse, and found all he could do was let his hands tremble against the table.

MARTHA DIDN'T QUITE KNOW how to hide her shock. In her decade living in Thatcham, she had heard all kinds of gossip about the Preston family, but never had it been suggested they erupted into this kind of violent conversation. It was unseemly; it was lowbrow; it was upsetting.

She couldn't quite say how it had come to be. She had expected tension between Lord Preston and Mrs. Caroline Chow, since he had confided in various ways how his relationship with his daughter was fractured. Yet one minute they were having a perfectly cordial conversation about the family, and the next, Caroline and Lord Preston were trading nasty barbs.

Her heart pounding in equal parts surprise and sympathy, Martha felt helpless as she watched Lord Preston, mumbling an apology for his manners, stalk to the fireplace. There, he took up the iron poker and stabbed at the fire a few times.

Martha knew what it was to have a child storm out—a child over whom one no longer held dominion. How many times, in those last few months before he eloped with Lady Imogen, had Lucas run out of the house as if chased by the devil? How many times had Martha regretted raising her voice or *not* raising her voice or calling him a brute or *not* calling him a brute? How many times had she wished him home so that she could take him in her arms like a babe and promise him that all would be well?

Lord Preston bent over the mantel and cradled his face in his forearms. Martha watched his shoulders heave as he sucked in breath. The sight of him—a man she knew to be steady and wise—so overcome by emotion snapped her into action. Turning to Jacques, the footman, who waited on the threshold for direction, she said, "You may clear the table, then take a half day. The rest of the household may take their half day, too." It was Sunday, after all.

Then, approaching Lord Preston as carefully as she would a skittish horse, Martha said, "Come, sir, let's retire to your study."

He didn't respond immediately, so she dared touch a hand to his back, between his shoulder blades, which still heaved violently.

"Please, Lord Preston, come along."

At his name, he lifted his head. Martha was relieved to discover he wasn't crying, just red in the face from catching his breath. He nodded and let her lead him out of the dining room, across the entrance hall, and into his study.

She locked the door behind them and, for good measure, folded her shawl across its bottom. The people of Northfield Hall were good people, but even the best people could be tempted to listen at the door after witnessing such a scene.

Lord Preston seated himself not at his desk but in the little clump of rococo settees near the bookshelves at the other end of the study. Martha joined him there, daring to sit beside him rather than on her own settee. She put a hand on the cushion between them in case he wanted to take it.

"I'm sorry for our terrible manners," Lord Preston said.

"Come now, I don't mind. It makes me feel as if I am part of the family."

"And eager to get out of it, I'm sure." He scrubbed a hand across his face, as if smoothing out his wrinkles would erase the conflict. "I let my temper get the best of me. I always seem to do that with Caroline."

Martha wished to touch him again, but she held back her fingers. Years ago, her sister had counseled her that falling a little in love with a person was not so bad a thing to do, so long as one didn't act on it. She could enjoy the excitement she felt in his company and embrace the energy it gave her each day, but as soon as it started tempting her to steal moments with him or to see if she could earn his esteem, then she must recognize the devil trying to lead her astray and resist.

Always before, Martha could rely on her marriage to keep her from giving in. Whether her *petit amour* (as she and her sister referred to it) was for the dairy farmer or the schoolteacher or the visiting dancing master, Martha had only to put her hand in Kenneth's to remember with whom her loyalties lay. And her heart—she had loved Kenneth, especially during their years in Tolpuddle.

But now he was gone, and Martha had no one to save her from temptation except herself. Which meant that she would *not* be grateful for this opportunity to sit next to Lord Preston *nor* relish the chance to earn his esteem.

She would feel only the sympathy of a friend who harbored no secret fantasies. She rebutted his self-rebuke: "I daresay Caroline wanted you to let your temper get the best of you, otherwise she wouldn't have provoked you so."

"Still, I am her father. I should be able to remain stalwart, especially when I can see her provocations as clearly as arrows."

"I did not know a father was not made of flesh and blood. Why, no wonder our government is full of fathers, if you are all able to remain stalwart even when greatly provoked!"

Her mirth earned her a little smile—and his eyes, connecting at last with hers. "All children provoke their parents. It is the parent's duty not to react."

"Yes, but when they are truly children, their attacks cannot wound us. Caroline is a fully grown woman now. She can wound just as deeply as any other adult." Thinking of that last time Lucas had slammed the door in Martha's face—after she had begged him not to write any more poems about Lady Imogen's perfect body—she added, "Perhaps even more deeply."

Lord Preston inhaled slowly, his eyes falling a little away from hers. "I am struck by how strange it is, Mrs. Bellamy, that we have only known each other for a handful of days. You seem to understand me as if we had been confidants for decades."

It was wicked, how her heart leapt. She forced herself not to beam. "I feel the same, sir."

"I'm not sure I have experienced such a..." His gaze lifted again as he searched for a word.

Hardly breathing, Martha volunteered, "Connection?"

"Connection. Yes. Have I ever experienced such a connection before?"

His words, meaningful as they were, hardly mattered to Martha, not compared to the way his whole being seemed to lean towards her.

She could not kiss him. She was a widow; he was a baron. This was the devil trying to tempt them into something that could never be.

But she could wallow in its gloriousness as it hovered between them like a possibility.

"I find myself afraid of saying the wrong thing," Lord Preston confessed.

Martha slid her hand a little closer to him on the cushion. "Perhaps we can count ourselves lucky for such a connection, sir."

"Lucky." He smiled. "Yes."

"And call ourselves friends," Martha dared add.

"Friends. Yes."

"And need not question it beyond that."

"Yes." At last, he took her hand in his. A soft grip, not unlike what any friend would offer another, except his touch made her whole body come alive. Lord Preston smiled. "Friends."

Martha wasn't sure she could have been more satisfied even if they had kissed.

Chapter Six

EMBARRASSED BY LOSING CONTROL of his emotions, Martin excused himself from Mrs. Bellamy, claiming that after the excitement, he needed rest. It was not a lie: he did feel exhausted to the bone, and when he shut the door of his drawing room on the rest of the world, he almost collapsed right there on the old sofa.

Even more than rest—which he took properly in his bed for half an hour—Martin needed solitude to compose himself.

He was disappointed in the way he had behaved with Caroline. Mrs. Bellamy was correct that he was wounded by his daughter trying so hard to disrupt their peace. But battles with Caroline were nothing new to Martin. This was, unfortunately, how it had been for almost three years now.

What disquieted Martin more was the exchange with Mrs. Bellamy.

The way his thoughts, in the aftermath of Caroline's departure, had caught in a loop of worrying what his guest must think.

The way her hand on his back had felt so perfectly comforting.

The way that, when she sank beside him on the settee, a part of Martin had yearned to pull her body against his. To touch her. To know her. To kiss her.

He had not felt such things since Lolly had died. Oh, he had noticed beautiful women who crossed his path—but with all the same distance as noticing a finely executed painting. And of course his body felt lust, yet never towards a specific person. He cared for himself with memories from his twenty years of bliss with Lolly.

He did not fixate on poor widows. Mrs. Bellamy would no doubt be horrified if she knew the fantasy that had flashed across his skin when their hands touched.

It was only because she was his first female confidante since Lolly. Martin had shared his worries about his children with Maulvi—and occasionally the Widow Croft, but only in Maulvi's presence, and she was too cheerful a woman to do anything except assure him a father knows best. True, when he and Caroline had first warred over Eddie, he had turned to Lolly's sister Charlotte for help—but Charlotte was like a well-meaning, overbearing, spoiled cousin to him. And while he supposed Caroline would point out that he had often relied on Mrs. Chow to care for the children, never had he confided in Mrs. Chow more than concerns for their physical health.

Mrs. Bellamy was the first friend with whom he had shared his deepest regrets *and* who was a woman. That was why he had for a moment been tempted to rip open that black cotton dress and sink his lips into her flesh. Not because it was what he *should* do, not even because it was what he actually *wanted*, but because it was instinct, like ducking when hearing a gunshot.

If he cultivated more women in his life to give him parenting advice, no doubt he would become immune to Mrs. Bellamy.

Alone in his bedroom, he saw to that terrible organ of his, fixing his mind on the memory of *Lolly's* breasts and *Lolly's* quim instead of thinking again of Mrs. Bellamy's breathless declaration that they were friends. When he was done—his body trembling with success, yet frustration still lingering—Martin washed his hands and face and changed into his old, patchy waistcoat. Had the servants not had their half day, he would have rung for leftovers from the failed dinner to be brought to his room and hidden the rest of the afternoon with a book.

As it was, he was *forced* to venture downstairs again. Not, as a lurid gossip columnist might imagine, because he sought out Mrs. Bellamy but because he was hungry.

He needed—wanted—space from her, not to find out if she still sat in the study, where he could still pin her to the couch to discover what her kiss tasted like.

He made it out to the kitchen and back into the rear corridor of the Hall without indulging his curiosity about Mrs. Bellamy's whereabouts. He told himself he would go straight upstairs—after all, she was likely resting in her own room.

Except, instead of going up the stairs, he found himself ducking into the study. To collect the committee report on revising the Corn Laws, which he still had to finish reading. That he happened to discover Mrs. Bellamy was, indeed, still sitting by the bookshelves was neither here nor there.

She had moved into a chair so that her back was to the door, and she did not stir at the sound of Martin's entrance. From the tilt of her head, Martin thought at first that she was asleep, and he told himself to retreat quietly so as not to wake her.

He crept forward instead.

She was not asleep. She studied a letter with her chin bent and her left hand clasped to her mouth, as if someone had died.

Martin's stomach flipped. Someone could have died.

"Have you had bad news?" he asked, forgetting that she did not know he had entered the room. She let out a strangled scream.

"I didn't mean to frighten you." Rushing to unburden himself first of the plate of food and the heavy committee report, Martin sank to his knees beside her chair and put his two hands on her arm to calm her. "Forgive me. I should have knocked at the door."

"Knocked at the door of your own study?" Her spare hand landed on top of his fingers, and she let out a shaky breath, clearly trying to paste over her emotions. "I should have removed to my room when you left. I remembered this letter that your daughter delivered and thought I would read it first, and since then, I forgot myself."

Caroline had said the letter was from Mr. Sebright—which couldn't mean that anyone had died, or Caroline would have shared that news, too. Unless Mrs. Bellamy's niece had finally written and the note had gone to her old address. Still holding onto her arm, Martin asked, "Is it news from your family?"

Shaking her head, she removed her fingers from his to hold the letter again. "A bill of dilapidations for the rectory."

Anger surged through Martin. Of course, it was not irregular for a new rector to ask the previous family to cover the cost of repairs to the parish house—yet he thought it in extremely poor taste considering Mr. Sebright counted Lord Harewood as a relation while Mrs. Bellamy didn't even have anywhere to live.

Besides, it had only been Mr. and Mrs. Bellamy living in the rectory for this past decade, with no children or grandchildren to wreak havoc. There couldn't be a great need for repairs.

"Are they asking for very much?"

For a moment, she seemed unable to answer, her eyes glued to the letter, her mouth stuck open on a word that would not come. At last, she said, "Whether it is very much or very little, I am afraid I cannot pay it."

She blushed—as if it were some stain upon her honor that she did not have the funds for such a bill!

Martin wanted to take her in his arms, and yes, he would kiss her, but more importantly, he would erase the shame from her being.

He settled for taking the letter from her. Moving into the chair beside hers—his knees could not bear to kneel for much longer—he read over its charges. New wallpaper to replace a patch in the living room. New thatching for the roof to fix a leak in the main bedroom. New tiling for the hearth in the kitchen.

This was not a good faith bill asking to share the burden of updating a rectory. This was highway robbery of a poor widow.

"This must be negotiated, Mrs. Bellamy. You do not bear the burden for all of these repairs."

She stared down at her feet, which were dainty in a pair of silk slippers she had probably bought as a bride. "I shouldn't like to cause trouble in the village over it. Perhaps I can pay in installments. I had planned to help my niece with her household, but I could take in sewing as well to pay off my debt."

Not for a second would Martin allow her to accept such a responsibility. "It shall not be so bad as all that. We'll talk with Mr. Sebright to sort this out. I promise you it shall not cause any trouble in the village."

She shook her head. "This is my challenge, not yours."

"Why should it be yours alone when I am ready and willing to help?"

With the same strength she had displayed in accepting his invitation to live at Northfield Hall, she lifted her chin and met his gaze directly. "You have already taken me in as a houseguest with no termination date. I will not turn into a leech, sir."

All questions of *shoulds* or *shouldn'ts*, all reasoning of why he felt this way or that, disappeared. Martin reached across the space between their chairs to touch her again, this time threading his fingers through hers. "I invited you to live here as a part of my duty. Now, I offer you my help as your friend. My dear Mrs. Bellamy, please, won't you allow me to be your knight in shining armor?"

How thrilling it was to even call her that: *my dear Mrs. Bellamy.* The words echoed in the air as she looked down at their intertwined hands, then back into his eyes. Martin couldn't breathe as he waited for her answer.

Her fingers tightened ever so slightly around his as she nodded. "If you so wish it, my lord."

"I do," he said, and though he knew he should let go of her hand, he didn't.

LORD PRESTON ARRANGED FOR them to ride to Thatcham the very next day in the family's carriage. As opposed to the gig, which was so well-used that it could have belonged to any prospering farmer in the neighborhood, the carriage could only be that of a lord. It boasted four wooden wheels with spokes painted to match the black lacquer of its body. The door bore the family crest in gold and red. When Boyle, the coachman, drove it round the sweep to fetch them, he wore a linen livery that Martha hadn't yet seen on the household servants.

"The gig is perfectly comfortable," Martha said to Lord Preston as he led her down the marble steps to the carriage. "I don't need such pampering as a coach-and-four."

"The horses need to stay in shape," Lord Preston replied, but from the way amusement crinkled around his eyes, Martha didn't believe him. This was a display of power—unusual in a man who spent most of his life trying to diffuse that power.

Inside, the carriage was even grander than Martha had imagined. The benches and walls alike were upholstered in fine wool—with a detailed pattern that depicted the façade of Northfield Hall—and cushioned so that she barely noticed when they started moving. From underneath the bench, Lord Preston withdrew a gleaming wooden box upon which she could rest her feet, as they didn't quite reach the floor. She discovered that it opened to hold a warming brick for winter rides.

As they rode to Thatcham, they discussed his recent correspondence with the Anti-Slavery Society about how to get votes for a bill to make slave trading piracy and why it would allow Britain to take even swifter action against the foreign ships they encountered carrying shipments of people to the Americas.

Martha asked a question that risked making her sound of the opposite view as him: "Why do we spend so much of our resources on chasing down slave traders of other nations? Wouldn't it be better to spend that energy abolishing slavery completely throughout the empire?"

A week ago, when she had first arrived at Northfield Hall, she would have kept the question in for fear of revealing her ignorance. But that was before they were friends. She knew Lord Preston would not hold her question against her, as Kenneth might have done, to remind her in a month or three that she had wondered such a thing. For Lord Preston, asking the question was far better than remaining in silence, pretending she understood.

"If only humans were guided by doing the good rather than the bad, then we could do that. Or rather, we wouldn't need to. Unfortunately, when we first abolished the slave trade, many British slavers started outfitting themselves as Americans or Spaniards to continue their business, not to mention all the establishments in Liverpool and Bristol that supply the slave trade who continue to participate in the shadows. If we do not make it impossible for *everyone*, then no one will quit the trade."

He accompanied the reply with a patient gaze, like a teacher gauging whether his pupil followed along.

Martha was distracted by those eyes—and how near he was on the opposite bench of the carriage, much closer than he ordinarily was across a table from her! Her heart was beginning to leap at each jostle of the carriage, few though they were, in hopes that his legs would knock against hers.

She tried to pin her thoughts to the topic at hand. "Do you think we shall ever succeed in abolishing slavery, even if we must continue languishing in the fight against the slave trade?"

On a sigh, Lord Preston looked out the window. "I have been fighting to abolish slavery since I came back to England in 1787. I thought it would have been long done by now. Still, I must believe it will be done. We must always keep fighting for what we know to be right, even when it seems impossible."

Martha imagined him saying such a thing in a London drawing room, surrounded by women who regularly rode in coaches like his, and how those ladies must covet him.

Why had he never remarried?

And what did he think of someone like her, who was too busy holding her own little life together to fight for anything larger?

When the carriage arrived at the rectory, which sat on a nice acreage a half mile off Chapel Street, dread settled around Martha like a winter cape. Lord Preston handed her down to the yard which used to be her yard. Boyle knocked on the door that used to be her door.

She had never loved this home, which felt more like a tomb where she and Kenneth awaited their final judgment. It had not been the place of casual visits, like the ones she received daily in Tolpuddle, nor did it hold happy memories to carry her back to better times. Yet returning to this rectory reminded her that she still did not have a home to replace it—and she might never have a house to call *hers* again.

Would she ever grow accustomed to how life could crumble from its foundations in an instant?

A housemaid—one whom Martha didn't recognize from Thatcham—answered the door. She blushed ferociously at the sight of the liveried coachman and carriage. "M-m-may I help you?"

"Lord Preston and Mrs. Bellamy for Mr. and Mrs. Sebright," Boyle intoned as imperiously as if they were calling upon a duke.

Martha wanted to object that all this pomp was unnecessary. But the farce had already begun, and it was too late to close the curtains.

"Won't you come in?" the housemaid said, ducking out of the doorway. "Oh, I shall see if they are at home to visitors."

Her accent was a lovely lilt, probably from the Irish community in Bristol, from whence the Sebrights had relocated. Martha busied her mind thinking about that instead of noticing they had moved her furniture around in the drawing room so that now the old chairs sat in corners while the settee hogged the space directly in front of the hearth.

Lord Preston did not sit, so neither did she. He withdrew the bill of dilapidations from his coat and lifted it to the light of the window to review it one more time.

Martha half wished she had never shown it to him. No, she couldn't pay it—but could she bear to have Lord Preston in this house, taking up a fight that wasn't his, simply because she was a weak woman who had not managed life properly?

Perhaps last week she would have welcomed his help, but now that she knew him—now that she craved his esteem—Martha wished he did not have so close a view of the true her.

Mr. and Mrs. Sebright rushed a little breathlessly into the room. When Martha had met them a week ago, they had been dressed in traveling costumes that had struck her as unnecessarily grand, and now Mrs. Sebright came in wearing a fine muslin day gown that could not possibly bear up to any kind of housework.

They did not truly rely on the living of the rectory, then—or they were willing to go into debt to swan about like a lord and lady.

Mr. Sebright bowed in greeting. "Lord Preston, I do apologize for keeping you waiting. We did not know to expect you. How honored we are to welcome you to our home." Belatedly, he nodded to her. "Ah, I'm afraid Betsy neglected to tell us about your companion."

Martha was so astonished that he didn't recognize her that she forgot her manners and could only gape at the man.

Lord Preston said, "I believe you had the pleasure of meeting Mrs. Bellamy when you arrived in Thatcham."

"Mrs. Bellamy, of course!" crooned Mrs. Sebright, diving forward to take Martha's hand as if they were the best of friends. "Please, sit, and we shall ring for tea."

The whole thing was too disorienting. Martha sat on the settee because someone put her there; she answered questions about the weather because she did not need a brain to do so; she pretended she was not there about the bill of dilapidations because they were pretending they had never sent it.

Across the hearth, on a sofa that had never belonged to Martha, Lord Preston seemed to be pretending, too. He even let them go through the trouble of presenting a tea set imported from China before saying, "No tea for me, thank you. I do not consume anything imported from beyond the isle of England."

Mrs. Sebright's cheeks flamed—as they should, since Martha had known that about the Preston family even when she lived in Tolpuddle.

"None for me either," Martha said, which she might not have done had they remembered who she was.

They declined the sugared biscuits, too, though Martha salivated a little at the sight of the sugar crystals baked on top. Mrs. Sebright, fussing, sent back the tea tray and called instead for warm milk and bread and cheese. "A rustic afternoon snack is good for everyone now and then, isn't it, Mr. Sebright?"

Rustic, when Martha and the rest of Thatcham regularly called such an offering a meal.

Lord Preston placed the bill of dilapidations on the table where so recently the decadent tea set had sat. "While we wait, perhaps we can discuss this bill that you sent to Mrs. Bellamy."

Mr. Sebright straightened beside Martha. He was a large man and took up most of the settee; with his posture erect, he loomed over her. He directed his words to Lord Preston. "As I'm sure you know, sir, it is a regular matter between the new rector and his predecessor's family. We ask nothing out of the ordinary, only for assistance in paying for the wear and tear on the rectory since Mrs. Bellamy moved in." At last, he looked at her, his red moustache twitching. "I'm sure Mr. Bellamy made similar negotiations with the Thistlemans when he first arrived in Thatcham."

Martha hadn't the slightest idea. That had been a year and a half after Lucas's death; she had thought herself on the other side of grief, but she knew now that she had still been slogging through fog. It wasn't until he had been gone five years or so that she finally began noticing sunlight again. When they had arrived in Thatcham, she had merely gone through the motions of unpacking her belongings, introducing herself to her new neighbors, and finding a hundred things to do so that at any moment she could be useful.

Lord Preston waved aside the idea that Kenneth might have sent the same bill to the grieving family of Mr. Thistleman. "I am sure you are a fair man, Mr. Sebright, and do not mind reviewing each charge with us."

The man squirmed in his seat. "Certainly, sir, though I must admit I find it highly irregular for a person such as yourself to take an interest in the matter. My cousin's husband, as you may know, is Lord Harewood, and he leaves such concerns as property negotiations to the parties involved."

A bold statement from a man who had been so eager to impress Lord Preston just moments ago. Martha's breath caught in her lungs. But Lord Preston only quirked his lips into a little smile. "As I'm sure you have heard by now, Mr. Sebright, I am unlike my peers. You will find I am very interested in the wellbeing of every person in the neighborhood." He leaned forward, his eyes drifting to Martha. "At the moment, of topmost priority is Mrs. Bellamy."

She had to look away or else surely the Sebrights would see that *her* interest far exceeded whatever was appropriate between a rector's widow and her patron.

The Sebrights reluctantly took them on a tour of the house to review each item in the bill. Even though she had studied the letter at least three times, there were items that Lord Preston asked about that she hadn't even noticed—such as retiling the hearth and reupholstering the furniture.

"As you have brought your own furniture, surely you would prefer to allow Mrs. Bellamy to take hers with her rather than require her to pay for you to keep using it," Lord Preston said as they debated over the settee by the hearth.

"It is not *hers*," Mr. Sebright insisted, "as by leaving it here, she indicated it was part of the rector's household."

Lord Preston looked to Martha. "Was it yours before you came to Thatcham?"

"Yes." It had been a wedding gift from her wealthy aunt, but Martha didn't like to think of all the memories associated with it. "I haven't any need for furniture now, so I left it behind."

"If you intend for us to use it, then it needs to be reupholstered," Mr. Sebright said.

"If you intend to make use of the gift donated to your household, then you may choose to reupholster it yourself," Lord Preston countered. "Otherwise, I know there are many families in Thatcham who would be happy to take it."

They looked at each patch of stained wallpaper, each uneven floorboard, even the scratch in the wood of the bedstead she had left behind, though they had moved it from the primary suite into a little attic room. Martha was equal parts charmed by Lord Preston's insistence that she not pay for anything beyond the necessary and horrified that he was making such an inspection of her life.

How could she be worthy of his notice now that he saw that only the mantle of rector's wife separated her from the poor farmers trying to eke out livings across the countryside?

She *wasn't* worthy of his notice. He gave her his friendship, nothing more. After all, she was an old woman. If he hadn't remarried one of the glittering women in London who could ride in his carriage without excitement, then he certainly wouldn't take up with a dusty old thing like herself.

In the end, she agreed to pay to replace the wallpaper, rethatch the roof, and fix the back door that didn't latch. Everything else would be the Sebrights' responsibility, if they wanted to make such improvements.

"I must confess I am surprised by this welcome," Mr. Sebright said as he walked them out to the carriage. "I have always been greeted with much ceremony and gladness when I have moved to new neighborhoods before, and then I was only a vicar. As your new rector, sir—"

Lord Preston cut him off. "You are not *my* rector, Mr. Sebright. You are the village's rector. They are under your care spiritually as they are under mine legally. As surprised as you are by this welcome, I am equally surprised that you are placing your own needs so high above someone else's."

The words were so cutting that Martha gasped aloud.

Lord Preston held out a hand to Mr. Sebright. "I do not mean to be harsh. Let us begin again in a few weeks on new footing."

Mr. Sebright glowed red, but he shook Lord Preston's hand.

Lord Preston waved Boyle onto the driver's seat and placed a hand on Martha's back to assist her into the carriage. The horses took off racing almost as soon as he shut the door. He let out a sigh, looked Martha in the eye, and shook his head.

"I'm sorry I let my temper get away from me like that. I hope you do not have to pay the consequences."

Strange, how it was the apology that, more than anything, stung Martha's eyes with tears.

CHAPTER SEVEN

Martin could have kicked himself for how poorly he had managed the afternoon.

He had envisioned it as a great triumph, one in which he would school Mr. Sebright in generosity while also displaying his prowess in negotiation to Mrs. Bellamy. Instead, he had insulted the Sebrights at least twice and now made Mrs. Bellamy cry.

Well, tear up. She was far too fastidious a woman to sob in his arms.

He didn't know why he had failed so spectacularly. This negotiation was nothing compared to the compromises he had supervised just this past year to reform the penal code. Yet in this, Martin had let fly the cold words that he ordinarily managed to keep from jabbing at his adversaries.

Perhaps it was because Mr. Sebright was such a pompous ass—and unlike the dukes in London who had their positions whether Martin liked it or not, *Martin* was the reason Sebright had the living. Thatcham was saddled with a rector more interested in tea sets than sermons because *Martin* had done a favor to Lord Harewood without researching the man's character. Mrs. Bellamy was suffering such humiliations as being asked to pay to reupholster her own sofa for someone else's use because *Martin* had failed to find a worthy rector for Thatcham.

And then, as they were leaving, Mr. Sebright had been so presumptuous as to reprimand *Martin* for his behavior.

Martin didn't want to be the kind of man who was insulted when an inferior acted out of turn. He didn't want to be the kind of man who believed in superiors and inferiors. Yet this was the world they lived in, and he *was* Sebright's superior in every respect, and Sebright dared to upbraid him for *his* conduct.

He shouldn't have let it rob him of good manners, but it had, and now as a result Mrs. Bellamy stared at him with red, wet eyes.

"If he gives you any further trouble, be sure to let me know," Martin said in an attempt to soothe her.

Turning towards the window, she pulled a handkerchief from her sleeve and dabbed at her eyes. "Oh, I am not concerned about that. There is not much more trouble that the Sebrights can give me."

Martin didn't know if he should pry. So often, the polite thing was to pretend the person in front of you wasn't crying.

But when the person in front of you was your friend? When she was someone with whom you had held hands for comfort?

She tucked the handkerchief away, her tears under control. "I didn't consider that it would be upsetting to revisit the house that was so recently mine. Grief comes in surprising manners, doesn't it?"

Grief. Of course. Because her husband had died six months ago. And Martin had dragged her back to the rectory to poke around every nook and cranny.

He would have done better not to play the knight in shining armor.

Leaning back against the carriage wall, he replied, "It does. Even now, fifteen years after Lolly died, I can be paralyzed just by the waft of a particular scent." Lilacs, usually, since they had been Lolly's favorites.

Mrs. Bellamy asked, "Would you tell me about Lady Preston?"

That was the question of someone practiced in comforting others. Yet Martin found himself reluctant to answer. He never minded talking about her with the children, but that was through the lens of her as a mother. He reminisced about her with Maulvi and Mrs. Chow, remembering anecdotes, without needing to explain to them the context of her personality. The whole Lolly, though—the delightful, stubborn, intelligent, independent woman he had loved—was a secret of his heart.

And she had died so long ago. The grief Martin carried now mingled with fear that if he could magically resurrect Lolly, she would not recognize the person he had become.

But he wanted to give Mrs. Bellamy a reply. "She had terrible allergies. In the springtime, she was always sneezing—and in such an unladylike manner." It was, of course, the spark that had forged their twenty-year union. "She was born in America, before it became independent, and would have stayed there as a revolutionary had her father allowed it. She almost returned to Boston instead of marrying me, in fact."

Mrs. Bellamy's brows rose. "I would be shocked save for how revolutionary you yourself are, sir."

"I am a reformer, to be sure—" Martin rushed to correct her "—but I do not go so far as to envision a revolution of government."

"Did Lady Preston?"

"No." Suddenly, Martin couldn't quite remember. He and Lolly had engaged in so *many* debates about policy and political theory and strategies to accomplish their goals. She had often played devil's advocate to push Martin to fully consider an issue. But had she ever truly advocated for a republic to replace the monarchy? Could he not remember, or had he not paid her attention if she did?

He did not want to pursue that line of thinking. A little defensively, he asked, "And what of Mr. Bellamy? I met him a few times, but I never had the pleasure of getting to know him fully. How would you describe him?"

The expression on her face—had it been curiosity? Sympathy?—disappeared, replaced by the nothingness that she had worn before their friendship blossomed. "He was a good man who tried to do his best by those around him."

And she must still be deep in her grief, if she needed to rely on such a platitude to reply. Martin remembered how hard it had been to bear even the mention of Lolly in the first year after her death, though of course she had occupied his every thought.

How foolish that he had been worrying these past few days about what Mrs. Bellamy thought of him. She wasn't thinking of him: her heart still belonged to her late husband.

Martin pushed away an ugly feeling that he feared was envy. "I'm sorry. I don't mean to dwell on so painful a topic."

"It is not painful for me to speak of him." She looked out the window, her eyes on something far away, as she selected her next words. "I don't think I was crying just now for Kenneth, but for the life I had that I can never have again."

And Martin felt as if she had reached into his soul to pluck out words he would never have found himself. Without knowing what he did, he crossed the carriage to sit beside her and take her hand in his.

She blushed. "Is that terrible of me, do you think?"

"It is human, which makes it both terrible and beautiful." He wrapped one palm beneath her hands and the other above them, holding onto the precious person she was. "I grieved Lolly deeply for years, and I still miss her, but what I grieve now is my children being young and my life being unlived and optimism about the years unfurling before me."

She leaned into his grasp. "I miss being someone. Even on my worst days, I was Kenneth's wife. He relied on me. The village relied on me. I was a help, not a burden. And now I'm—" Those tears flooded her eyes again. "I'm an old woman that Mr. Sebright did not recognize, even though he turned me out of my home just last week."

He couldn't help it: he cupped his gloved fingers around her chin. "You are someone, Mrs. Bellamy. You are someone spectacular."

Her lips parted, but no words came. They were both leaning in, and, though a dim warning somewhere in Martin's head tried to stop him, with a soft jolt of the carriage, they kissed.

He had not shared a romantic kiss with anyone since Lolly died, and oh, how that first touch flooded his body with youth. Mrs. Bellamy tasted of white wine—or what he remembered of white wine from before he gave up Continental imports—a delicious, dry sweetness that he wanted to inhale with every breath. He couldn't help but linger, especially not when her hand slid behind his ear to hold him close and her thumb swept across his cheek in a tender caress. When the carriage jostled, he grasped her waist and remembered what it was to hold someone against his body. Bliss blanketed his mind, quieting his thoughts, so that he felt only a fuzzy joy of lips, tongue, fingers, knees.

He had told himself all these years he did not need a woman's touch.

He had not considered how much he wanted it.

And he especially wanted *this* woman. The woman whose lips he plundered and whose skin set his own on fire. Mrs. Bellamy, his friend, who somehow knew his deepest regrets and still admired him.

Her breath grew ragged. So did his. Their hands remained on his neck, her waist, his chest. Their clothes did not loosen, her hair did not shake free from its coiffure. His cock, harder than it had been in decades, did not approach her skirts. Yet the kiss continued, growing more delicious with every second, and Martin began to believe it would never end.

Then the carriage slowed. The voices of workers calling to each other in the fields filtered through the windows. A horse neighed.

And Martin remembered decorum. Propriety. The fact that Mrs. Bellamy was a widow in his care, not a wife to be enjoyed.

The pleasure of kissing her was almost too strong for his principles to break through—but Martin had lived six decades as a man of principle. Somehow, he withdrew his hands from her waist. He loosened hers from around his face and placed them in her lap. Worst of all, he forced his mouth to separate from hers.

They smiled at each other. And their fingers, devils that they were, intertwined. It was only at the last moment, when the carriage entered the sweep in front of Northfield Hall where anyone from the household could see them, that Martin returned to the bench opposite hers.

What a wonderful kiss.

How terrible that he had let it happen.

How horribly he already wished it could happen again.

As Boyle opened the door to help them out, Mrs. Bellamy said, "Thank you for your assistance this afternoon, sir."

"I am at your disposal, Mrs. Bellamy."

She smiled, and he smiled, and Martin knew it would be up to him to resist her from here on out.

Chapter Eight

Only a fool would pursue a love affair with a lord of the realm.

Apparently, Martha was a fool.

It had been one thing to romanticize Lord Preston while acting as his temporary secretary. Imagining deeper meaning in his compliments and suggestive desire in his looks had been a way of lightening her days—making her feel young again, even.

But now he had kissed her.

Martha didn't know how to keep her head on straight after such a kiss.

She would have kept kissing him forever. Even after Lord Preston pulled away, there had been such desire glimmering in his expression that Martha had nearly thrown herself back onto his mouth to resurrect their embrace.

But the carriage had stopped, and they had descended as if they were only a lord and his dependent, and Martha could not even keep holding his hand. Lord Preston excused himself to examine the roof of the stable.

Martha was too muddled with desire to do anything but retreat to her room, claiming to the maid Renee that she needed a lie-down.

Of course, she couldn't sleep. Alone in her room, she shut the door—but did not lock it, in case Lord Preston miraculously decided he needed to enter. She left the curtains open, too, though he would have to climb a tree to look in. She didn't care about reason or reality; her body was alive like a young bride's, and she wanted to put it to use.

She washed her face, hands, and thighs in the basin by the window. Unbuttoning her sturdy gown, she exchanged it for her linen dressing robe, tied at the waist over corset and petticoats. She unpinned her hair so it fell in silver waves down her back. She even dabbed on the London perfume she saved for special occasions—though she knew her bed partner would never come.

Lord Preston had kissed her, and that was enough fuel for her to imagine him coming to her after his errand in the stables. She pictured him staring up at the roof with a cock stand, waiting desperately for his chance to get away, only the stable master was talking his ear off and dear Lord Preston couldn't very well say *Mrs. Bellamy is waiting for me to fuck her.*

Martha had always delighted in the dirty words when unwrapped in the privacy of her boudoir. In company, they were vulgar; in an embrace with Kenneth, they were aphrodisiacs. She wanted to be fucked, she wanted her cunny to be toyed with, she wanted to fill the room with tits and pricks and bawdels. Just thinking of the words kept Martha's lust alive. Laying back on her mattress, she spread her legs wide and murmured them to herself as she licked her fingers and flicked her own pussy back and forth. "Fuck me like a whore, Lord Preston," she whispered—and pretended he was walking through the door to find her ready for him. "Put that big cock inside me, sir." And imagined a girth and length like never before filling her. "Rut me as fast and hard as you can."

The words in the air, even though she said them to herself, carried her to ecstasy. Martha muffled her cry with her pillow.

A wise woman would let that be the end of it. Nothing good came of a sixty-two-year-old widow chasing after a baron.

You are someone spectacular.

Martha found it difficult not to be a fool. The next morning, after taking both supper and breakfast in her room, she reported to the study in her widow's weeds with her hair braided too tightly as a reminder to herself to behave. Lord Preston stood from his desk to greet her but did not meet her eyes, instead handing her a stack of correspondence. "If you are willing, would you please decline these invitations for me?"

Of course, a small part of her had hoped he would sweep her into his arms once more, but she could not blame him for trying to put the kiss behind them. *He* was no fool. Martha schooled her body not to react as she took the letters from him, and she successfully avoided grazing her thumb against his.

Her breath still shortened, her heart racing, just from being near him.

A woman couldn't help being a fool; she could only endure it until her body released her from its daydreams at last. Martha endured by writing out the rejections Lord Preston requested; by trimming her pens and organizing her desk; by not complaining when he excused himself to review crop plans with the farmers. If she found herself analyzing the looks he gave her, she pinched her thigh and refocused on the task at hand. If she indulged herself by making a witty comment to catch his attention, she paid penance by noticing the excuses he found *not* to take luncheon with her.

The kiss would fade into a memory—no, a dream!—if she only bided her time.

It was the afternoon of her third day of enduring when Lord Preston groaned from behind his desk. Martha whirled around, expecting to find he had sliced his hand open with a penknife, to see that he had pushed away from his desk and stalked to the bay window, frustration lining his face.

"Is something the matter?" she asked.

He exhaled in a slow hiss through his teeth. "Reality frustrates me."

It was far too philosophical an answer for his agitation. If Martha wanted to overcome her infatuation, she knew she should turn away now and let him soothe himself. But what if he meant the reality of *her* frustrated him? And if he did, was it that she was present and he could not have her that frustrated him, or that she remained present when he had made it clear he did not want her?

She asked, "To which reality do you object at the moment?"

"Financial reality." He glared back at his desk, as if it were the devil himself. At the same time, he ran a hand through his thick hair—and Martha had to remind herself not to let lust levitate her away from the conversation. "The Ladies' Society for the Relief of African Slaves has lost their major funder, and they have asked me to make up the difference so they may continue operating. But the only funds I have available are required here to expand the living quarters."

It wasn't fair of her, but Martha couldn't help smiling. He wasn't frustrated with her at all. "We common folk like to imagine that you peers do not have any financial woes, but you're just like the rest of us, balancing your budget between what you need and what you want."

Lord Preston echoed her smile with a shy quirk of his lips. "Money is, unfortunately, a universal evil."

It was the fact that he was looking at her again without any of the polite shields he had used these past few days that spurred Martha to hold out her hand for the letter in question. "Then a little commonsense budgeting must surely be a universal skill. Let me see if there isn't a solution available for you."

He handed her the letter. In fact, he did more than hand it to her: he walked over to place it in her hand and remained by her side while she read it.

His presence made her mind flutter, so she had to read the letter a few times before it made sense.

"They need five thousand pounds to keep operating through next year," Lord Preston said, "and I haven't five thousand pounds to spare."

Martha got to the end of the letter, where she found the writer had predicted this problem. "No, you haven't, but you have a following of good people who are willing to take your direction." She pointed out the relevant paragraph to him. "Mrs. Brockway suggests you ask some of your friends to help raise the necessary funds. Do you have a hundred pounds available to start a pool of donations?"

"And fifty friends?"

She raised an eyebrow. "Surely some of your friends are even wealthier than you."

Now his smile was unadulterated. "You have turned my mountain back into a molehill."

"As you did for me with Mr. Sebright. It is what friends do." She said it to remind herself that they were nothing more than friends—not so that this interchange would lead to another kiss.

But when he stared into her eyes and said, "You are incomparable, Mrs. Bellamy," she found she didn't have the strength to endure it.

"You mustn't compliment me like that if you don't intend to do anything about it."

The man looked at her with such astonishment that Martha almost wondered if she had made the whole carriage ride up. She lifted her chin as high as when her mother used to stack books upon her head.

"You kissed me. Did you think I would forget?"

Lord Preston took a step backward. His hand clapped across his heart. "I owe you an apology. Multiple apologies. First, for the...and then, for handling the aftermath poorly. I am sorry. I am ashamed of myself, which is my best excuse for why I have been so eager to act as if..."

Martha waited. As if *what*? As if he had never been so idiotic as to kiss her? As if he had never kissed a woman as old as she? Or as if he had never been swept up in a wave of feelings, as she had been?

He looked up instead of completing the sentence. Whatever he saw in her eyes made him straighten and he said more sincerely, "I have failed you. You are right; I should have explained myself. I'm sorry."

Martha's heart thudded a little painfully. What she had wanted was for him to have followed her up to her bedroom, not to have explained his reasons for not doing so.

But she would accept the explanation, if she couldn't have him. "You may explain yourself now."

He blinked at her, cheeks red.

"You need not worry about injuring my feelings," Martha said, though it was a lie. "If you regret what transpired because I am unappealing, I will not run crying to the gossips that you have broken my heart. I only want to know the truth so I may reckon with it."

"I do not find you unappealing. How could you think I find you unappealing?" Lord Preston fell to his knees before her chair and took her hand. "You are—that is to say—I find you very appealing, Mrs. Bellamy. That is why I must not impose myself upon you. We are not...I..." He stared down at her fingers. "This is the type of situation that fathers warn their daughters against. I do not want to do wrong by you."

It was strange to hear herself referred to as a daughter, as if she were an errant youth swept up by unwise passion.

As if she were as reckless as Lucas.

"I did not find our kiss an imposition."

Lord Preston's breath landed in a rush on her hand. "But what does a kiss lead to?"

And Martha knew she was a fool for pressing on with this conversation. She was a respectable woman; her husband was only seven months in the grave; she knew better than to pursue an illicit love affair with a baron who could never marry her.

But, after all, that wisdom was for women who wanted husbands. "I am no virgin, sir, nor am I in danger of falling pregnant. Are you so faithful a man that you are shy of fornication?" Kenneth, who had prided himself on being a practical rector, had counseled that a little fornication before marriage kept bad unions from tying people together for life, and most people Martha knew did not actually pay too close attention to the boundaries of matrimony.

Then she remembered the mistress waiting for him in London. "Are you being faithful to someone else?"

His brow knitted together, and his gaze at last lifted to meet hers again. "I am a man who lives by my principles. What funds I do have go into Northfield Hall. I do not keep a mistress. I never have."

There was an anger lacing his reply that suggested men who did keep mistresses lacked moral fiber. Which gave Martha enough hope to smile. "Is that it? I do not hope to be kept by you any more than you are keeping me already by hosting me at Northfield Hall."

"You owe me nothing for that."

"This isn't about what is owed. This is about what is wanted." She cleared her throat because even now, she wasn't sure she was brave enough to say it aloud. "I only want to be your lover."

He gripped her fingers as if the world would fall apart if he let go. "It isn't the right thing to do."

"But why not?"

His dark eyes flickered all over her face. "Everyone knows it isn't right. A man should only do such things with his wife."

"Why?" She let herself look at those lips, which she had spent so many hours daydreaming about. "Explain it to me, Lord Preston. Give me as cogent an argument as you made to Parliament for penal reform."

His tongue darted out to wet his lower lip. He adjusted his fingers, his thumb sweeping across the bare expanse of the back of her hand. Martha felt every twitch to her core, but she waited.

"It skews the dynamics of a community. It upends who owes whom what. It will make me consider you in decisions in which you should carry no weight."

"In other words, it threatens that great natural order that you wholeheartedly believe in?"

Lord Preston scraped his gaze across her face. "Why are you torturing me so?"

The words lit Martha on fire.

He thought she was spectacular.

He considered her incomparable.

And he wanted her so badly that he was torturing himself to keep from having her.

"Because you have been a bad student," she whispered, as wickedly as she might say a dirty word, "and you have not sufficiently considered alternate perspectives on this topic."

He rasped back, "How am I to consider alternate perspectives?"

To which Martha replied: "Lock the door."

Chapter Nine

Martin locked the door.

All three of them: the one to the foyer, the one to the rear corridor, and the one to the side gallery in which residents sometimes sat to read the newspapers.

He locked the doors, and he was alone with Martha, who watched him with dark, expectant eyes. He thought he might die if she didn't give him another command. His heart was beating wildly, his blood pumping through every artery of his body with a force it hadn't known for decades.

Rising from her chair, she stretched out her hand. Martin closed the distance between them to take it. Her fingers were warm and sure. She tugged him as close as they had been moments before. "You are going to kiss me now," she whispered, "and you are not going to feel any guilt about it, because I am asking you to do it and because you want to do it."

He did want to do it. All he had wanted for these past three days was to consume her—even, at supper, imagining himself licking the mutton sauce from her fingers. Martin lifted her hands to his lips and kissed her smooth nails. He glanced up to see if he had earned a reprimand, but her eyes were darker than ever, her lips parted on a breath that never became words. He moved his way up her knuckles—small, then big—before flipping her hands so he could press his mouth to each wrist, one after the other. He tasted this soft skin with his tongue. She was a briny cream, a heady rose.

Martin wanted to kiss her lips, and she had asked him to, so he circled his arms around her waist to bring her close and dipped his mouth to hers.

They did not waste time pretending they were polite or demure. Mrs. Bellamy opened her mouth to his, and their tongues touched like the devils they were. Martin heard his breath become ragged. He bent down to her, craving every inch of her, and when her mouth wasn't enough, he bundled her in his hands to lift her against his body.

Except, of course, she was no dainty debutante, nor he a well-formed rake. He lifted her a half-inch from the ground before his back objected painfully. Mrs. Bellamy pushed her feet back to the floor, glaring at him again with hungry impatience. "Take me to the sofa."

He led her to the deeper, darker part of the study where book-shelves towered instead of sunlit windows. Here, not long ago, he had held her hand in friendship and told himself that it was enough.

Could he ever have believed that lie?

He meant to seat her on the sofa, as she had commanded. Except her hips were so inviting beneath his palms, and their lips had been separated for too long. She turned to look up at him the very moment he decided he had no more patience, and that was all it took for him to push her against the bookshelf for another kiss.

She wanted this from him. She would get it: every terrible, carnal desire, including lifting her once more—this time, using the power of his legs instead of his back—to prop her against the hip-level shelf that housed records of the estate. Martin could press his cock against her thigh now, stealing her soft warmth through their clothes. He moved his hands to her breasts, seizing them despite the corset that protected their shape, and took her right earlobe with the tips of his teeth.

"Oh yes," she said on a breath that was far too tense to be a sigh. "Oh, be ruthless with me. Tease me—even when I want you to stop."

So Martin lingered on that ear, making it wet with his tongue, scraping it with his teeth, blowing on it with soft breaths, until Mrs. Bellamy writhed against his cock so much that he couldn't concentrate any longer.

He slipped a hand down to her ankle, which had coiled around his thigh. "What should I do next, mistress?"

Her hands gripped around his neck. "Find out if I am wet enough for you yet."

How he had been hoping that would be her command. Martin slid his fingers up the inside of her skirts, tracing the skin of her calf, her knee, her thigh, until he found the coarse hair protecting her hot, greedy folds. They were moist but not so wet that his hand became slick, and so Martin pressed his thumb into her apex and asked, "What do you want now?"

"Your tongue," she gasped, trembling a little in his grip, and Martin tortured her further by kissing her mouth first.

Then, sinking to his knees, he hooked her legs over his shoulders to share her weight with the bookshelf and positioned his tongue on her quim. Here, she tasted of salt water, like a tonic for a sore throat, and he partook of her like an ailing man. Desperately. Lustily. Demandingly. He explored her geography with his tongue and learned her desires as she panted against the bookshelves. "Stay right there," she commanded at one point, "and don't slow down. No, don't speed up, either. Just like that. Stay right there. Fuck me with your tongue."

And so he did. He was her pupil, the Socrates to her Aspasia, and from her he would learn why this was neither corrupt nor evil.

Or he would give over his soul to the devil, once and for all, and at last live free of the fear of failure and the chains of guilt.

She came, not in a burst or shudder, but in a light, surprised cry of, "Lord Preston!" Martin only knew she had achieved ecstasy—or he had delivered her to it—because her whole body relaxed, and she sighed, "Oh, well done."

His own need had abated in the task of worshipping her on his knees, but as he rose back to his feet, his cock flooded with intense desire. As if *he* were an appendage of *it*, designed only to get him inside her hot vagina.

Mrs. Bellamy met his gaze with those dark, hungry eyes once more. "Do you think me ready for you?"

"Perhaps some pomade de pimpernel would help," he admitted. "I have one for my hands, if you would like it."

It was in a drawer in the table beside the sofa. Mrs. Bellamy sniffed it before she lay back on the cushions and, spreading her legs, massaged it inside her body.

The sunlight barely reached this dark corner of the study, yet Martin couldn't look away from the display of her quim, like a case of jewels against the backdrop of her widow's weeds.

She commanded, "Take off your trousers."

He did—his trousers, his stockings, his boots, and his coat, so that all he wore in the name of modesty was his long white shirt.

His conscience reminded him this was a bad idea. He would not want his children to do this. He would not want another man to take advantage of Mrs. Bellamy in such a way.

She caught his hand in her fingers. "Lord Preston."

He liked her fingers so very much. "Surely you mustn't call me that now."

"What name should I use? Your Christian name?"

Lolly was the last person to have called him Martin. But she was his wife, not just his lover, and a woman of the same rank, besides.

If he gave Mrs. Bellamy leave to use that name—that was something entirely different from letting lust rule for an afternoon. "Preston," he said. "It's what my friends call me."

"Preston." She kissed his fingertips. "May I touch you?"

Confused—they were already holding hands, after all—he nodded, and she wrapped her palm lightly around his shaft. How heavenly it was—or was it evil because it was such a wonderful temptation?

Martin would already reap the consequences of this afternoon. He might as well give in completely.

"Would you think me very wicked if I kissed it?" she asked, her mouth already close to his cock. He had no breath with which to reply. He shook his head.

She did more than kiss it. She took it in her hot, wet mouth and worshipped it the way he had just done her quim: with long, smooth motions; with fast flicks across its tip; with her hand teasing one part and her tongue another. But she only plunged him into the pool of ecstasy without giving him a chance to swim: soon, she withdrew her mouth and gazed up at him. "I want to have you inside me. Do you want that, too?"

Oh, how badly he did. "Yes."

"Then take me." Lying back, she spread her legs once more. Her quim was slick from the pomade and her own desire. "We are two old adults. We won't get confused."

She didn't want anything from him but this. And he—Martin didn't know what he wanted other than to complete this moment. There was no more time for doubts, only time for doing.

He climbed onto the sofa so that his knees balanced on either side of the cushions. Her ankles wrapped around his torso, bringing him close, and Martin leaned down to kiss her mouth once more. Compared to everything else they had done, it now felt innocent, this tender exchange of desire. A reminder that this was not just a woman with a quim, but Mrs. Bellamy—a woman he admired, who he hoped in turn admired him.

And then her hand was on his cock again, guiding it to her entrance. He slid in slowly, watching her for signs of discomfort. Halfway in, he lost conscious thought, overwhelmed almost to a swoon by the sensation of being swathed in another body. His hips acted of their own accord. She met his movement beat for beat. This was not tender: this was animalistic rutting, their breaths getting shorter, their bodies getting frantic, their thoughts replaced by instinct. Martin curled over Mrs. Bellamy, his mouth buried in the hair coming loose from her thick braid, and gave himself over to the great blankness of fucking.

"Oh Preston," she whispered in his ear, "yes, just like that."

He didn't like the new name, but he came anyway, in an amazing eruption of bliss that he had entirely forgotten was possible.

Wrapped around her in recovery, he returned to himself to find a man who had fucked the poor widow in his care, and he wondered if he would ever forgive himself.

MARTHA HOPED HER HEART was not about to burst. Her pulse was racing so fast that it tapped against the skin of her wrist and neck. She wondered if Lord Preston could feel it as he draped over her, spent.

She hadn't had a vigorous fuck like that in years, and she wasn't sure her heart could still withstand it. So she lay quietly, eyes closed, hand on Lord Preston's back, to let her breath return to her lungs.

What a thrilling thing it was, to be the object of desire of *one's* object of desire. She could hardly believe that after these days of pushing her away, he had kissed her again. Kissed her and shoved her against bookshelves and made her forget her own name with the delights of his tongue!

If her heart *did* burst, then so be it, for she was happy.

Eventually, Lord Preston stirred, shifting his weight so he could sit at the end of the sofa instead of curling his whole body around hers. Stripped to only his white linen shirt, he looked both younger—his thighs were remarkably thick and strong!—and more vulnerable. Martha's instinct was to wrap her arms around his neck again, but she resisted.

She wasn't his wife, after all. It was not her place to shield him from the cold any more than it was hers to confess affection.

"Are you—?" Awkwardly, he touched her bare calf. "Did I hurt you?"

She wondered why he would worry he had. "Quite the opposite," she assured him, pulling herself up to sit in a position mirroring his. She had never disrobed, and so her skirts fell back over her lap as if nothing had happened. She tried to ease his tension by returning to their earlier farce. "That was a very thorough and satisfactory examination of the opposing viewpoint."

He smiled. It was a trick of the heart that now, post-coitus, he was a hundred times handsomer than the handsome he had already been. But it was true: Martha felt she could gaze upon nothing but his smile and be happy for the rest of her life—without food, without water, without anything but him right there at the end of the sofa.

"And what do we do now?" he asked.

Confess our admiration for each other. Promise to do this again tomorrow. Admit that we haven't felt like this in ages. Martha bit back all her honest replies. Her heart was surging with feeling, but that didn't make any of it true.

It wasn't as if she wanted to marry Lord Preston. Nor become his mistress, kept in an elegant house in London to always await his visit. Nor did she want him to say he loved her—for how could he, after so short an acquaintance?

She tried to laugh off the question. "To tell you the truth, sir, I have never carried off an affair like this before, so I haven't a clue. Have you?"

She meant: Did he have an idea what they might do next? He answered a different question: "I have never done, either. I haven't...you are the first woman I have kissed since Lolly died. The first woman I have even wanted to kiss."

Lord Preston did not look at her as he admitted this, his eyes dropping instead to his hands, which bunched the hem of his shirt nervously.

Martha did her best to contain her astonishment. "And here I thought the upper class was incapable of celibacy."

"Only the most elite of us," he said, smiling again.

But the words ended there because neither of them knew what to do next. Her back aching, Martha shifted on the sofa to find a more comfortable position, resisting the urge to scoot close beside him.

Lord Preston reached out and took her hand in that courtly way of his. "This does not change your welcome here at all. You must consider yourself my guest until you have sorted out your new situation with your family. I don't want you rushing away because I have importuned you."

There he went again, assuming he had somehow injured her when she had explicitly asked him to take her in his arms. "You did not importune me." To make her point, she used the name he had given her. "*Preston*. We both wanted this." But she would not allow herself to become a nuisance. "Perhaps I wanted it more than you. Should I keep to myself until I hear from my niece?"

He looked her in the eyes as he shook his head. "You did not want this more than I did."

Peace settled in her heart with those words. Martha tightened her fingers around his. "Then while I wait to hear from my niece, what do you want next?"

Gravely, as if confessing the worst sin, he admitted, "I want to do that again. Perhaps in a bed."

"Yes. I would like that too." She almost lost her breath from the words alone.

"Then, we may consider ourselves friends just like before."

Just like before and nothing like it. "Friends of a deeper nature," she agreed.

"A deeper, secret nature."

"A deeper, secret, natural nature."

Lord Preston smiled and kissed her fingertips. "The most natural nature there is, my dear Mrs. Bellamy."

And while she desperately wanted to bid him call her Martha, she resisted, because they had to remain friends just like before.

Chapter Ten

FRIENDSHIP, IT TURNED OUT, could be intoxicating.

By day, Martin remained Lord Preston, puzzling through decisions about who should get what investments and where his time should be spent in advocacy. He ordered repairs for the textile works and the stables. He put off the question of the cottages for another week or two. He corresponded about the slave trade bill. All of this he did with Mrs. Bellamy by his side, those intriguing reading glasses perched on her nose, their roles clearly defined as baron and secretary.

By night, he stole into Mrs. Bellamy's boudoir and turned that friendship into something salacious.

By day, he tried his best not to imagine kissing her fingers or fantasize about pinning her atop his desk.

By night, he freed her body from its clothes and explored every inch of her bare skin with his.

It was wicked, it was wrong, it was everything he would caution a sensible person against—and he was as addicted to it as a drunk to his gin.

It was not just her body that Martin wanted to consume. He wanted to know every inch of Mrs. Bellamy's soul. What her parents had been like, how many siblings she had grown up with, what she loved best to eat, what rules she had broken as a youth. He wanted to ask how she had met her late husband and how deeply they had loved each other; he wanted to know if her husband had made her buckle in pleasure the way Martin did and if her husband had also discovered the secret spot on the back of her knee that could make her moan with desire.

He restrained himself from asking such questions. This was a friendship, not a love affair. They both knew it would end when Mrs. Bellamy's niece wrote to invite her to stay.

Martin felt it would be easier for both of them if he kept his curiosity at bay.

As the autumn harvests finished, Martin arranged a visit to the property east of Northfield. The grim nabob who had held onto the property these past fifteen years had died, and the new owner, his nephew, was eager to lease it for someone else to take on its fallow fields. If Martin brought it under Northfield's care, he would add two hundred acres, access to more of the river, and a rocky portion which could potentially sustain construction for lodging houses and cottages.

By this point, it was self-evident that Mrs. Bellamy would accompany him—and not only because of how intensely Martin missed her if he spent more than an hour or two away from her side. In the month that she had been at Northfield Hall, she had proven herself to be the steady head who listened to facts and figures while Martin's worries swept him away from reality.

She wasn't quite a replacement for Maulvi—who knew every inch of the soil, every person's name, and every crack in the façade of Northfield Hall—but she was picking up some role Martin had never realized was vacant. Perhaps all secretaries did more than copy out correspondence.

Perhaps Mrs. Bellamy was special.

They rode in the coach-and-four to meet with the estate agent. He was a local man whom Martin had encountered now and again on various Thatcham business, and as he took them around the property, he emphasized all the ways it could help the project of Northfield Hall. "These fields would do well with peas and beans, if I may say so, sir," and, "You can see this is a prime pasture for another flock or two of sheep."

"It will take a year or two to restore these fields, will it not?" asked Mrs. Bellamy at one point as the agent waxed on about the fertility of the land.

The man reluctantly admitted it was so.

"And there are no houses at the ready for the farmers who will need to do the work."

To this the agent did not agree as easily, since he had shown them a set of dilapidated sheds that had supposedly once housed tenant farmers.

She said with just enough guile for Martin to detect that she was playing the role of an ignorant old woman, "When rectories change hands, we widows must lay out some of our own money to pay for the new tenants' repairs. Is there no such arrangement between a landlord and his long-term lessee?"

The agent humored her with a condescending reply. "These matters are more complicated as the property size increases."

Martin resisted the urge to draw Mrs. Bellamy into the protection of his arm. "The specifics will be complicated by the solicitors, no doubt, but the principle remains. I wonder what accommodations Mr. Lyne can offer, either in terms of a discounted rate in the first years or a stipend for improvements, to make the lease a better investment for me."

"I'm sure Mr. Lyne is willing to consider such a thing, so long as he is earning a fair value from the property."

In the carriage on their way home, Martin reviewed the negotiation with Mrs. Bellamy. "You are most astute, my dear secretary."

"I'm sure you already had some kind of discounted lease in mind," she said humbly.

The truth was that it hadn't occurred to Martin. He had taken the offer at face value: either he could sign the hundred-year lease at two thousand pounds per year, or he could decide that was too rich and let someone else move in as his neighbor. He had even gone so far as to wonder if he could convince an ally to lease the property and work out a barter system with Northfield to supplement their yields.

If he had property available to lease, he would price it at what it was worth, not at what he wanted to earn from it. But, of course, Mr. Lyne was a worldly man, not necessarily a fair one, and Martin had to remember that every point of the agreement could be negotiated.

"Do you think it is worth the investment?" he asked Mrs. Bellamy, eager for her honest opinion. Though they were alone in the carriage, he resisted the urge to reach for her hand. During the day, she was his secretary; it was only at night that he allowed himself to trespass the lines of respectability.

"It answers many of your prayers, most especially for space to build more lodging."

"For a substantial cost."

Mrs. Bellamy arched an eyebrow. "I can think of only one solution that would come at no cost, sir, and that is to declare you have reached the limit of the number of people Northfield can sustain and that no others will be admitted."

Martin hated to admit that the idea had occurred to him—even though he had dismissed it immediately. "The cost of that on my soul would greatly outweigh the financial savings."

The smile this reply earned him made Martin want to steal a kiss from her. He would save it for later, for when they were man and woman instead of lord and secretary.

But Mrs. Bellamy seemed to make no such distinction. Lifting the skirts of her traveling costume, she crossed the carriage to sit beside him. His body reacted instinctively; his skin heated, his lips tingled, and his cock began to stir. "You don't give yourself enough credit that you will naturally find your way to the right solution."

Martin fought to keep his mind attached to reason. "Only because I know how gravely I have failed in the past."

Her hand landed on his chest, just above his heart. "Your record is surely better than those who do not try to do the right thing at all."

He wondered if she could feel his heart thudding through the layers of his wool suit. Then he wondered why he was wearing so many clothes.

Her thoughts must have followed along the same track, for her spare hand tugged at the top button of her neckline. "I'm feeling rather hot all of a sudden. Would you mind if I remove my cape?"

It was a bad idea. The carriage had its natural jostle, yes, but Boyle would surely notice if it suddenly took on a rhythm of its own. Not to mention, anything could happen along the ride—a busted wheel, a horse with a stone in its hoof, a flock of sheep blocking the road—that might require them to step out of the carriage at a moment's notice. The smart thing to do was wait for nighttime, when they could lock Mrs. Bellamy's door and enjoy each other in relative peace.

But Martin's blood responded to the scent of Mrs. Bellamy. With only the slightest encouragement, he unbuttoned his trousers. He pulled Mrs. Bellamy's soft curves onto his lap. With her lips now above him, they shared fast, messy kisses. Under her skirts, he could feel the raw heat of her quim against his freed prick—which was now achingly stiff. She wouldn't be wet enough for him to enter her, not after so little time and with no pomade to assist. Martin snaked his hand between her legs to work her with his thumb and fingers. Her quim was plump, like the rest of her, and once activated with desire, it rose sturdily to receive its pleasure. Mrs. Bellamy rested her forehead against his as he worked her ridges, her breath growing shorter and shorter as his hand moved faster and faster. They had been lovers for long enough that Martin knew her rhythm, and in no time, she was gasping in his ear.

The carriage turned, which Martin knew meant they were joining the main road to Thatcham, and Boyle called out a greeting to some vehicle coming their way.

Martin had no need to stop and chat with a passerby. He could ignore them entirely or simply raise a hand in acknowledgment as their horses pulled them in opposite directions.

He panicked anyway. He yanked himself straight from underneath Mrs. Bellamy. Giggling at him, she pulled away—but instead of retreating to her proper bench, she fell to her knees on the floor.

"What are you doing?" he hissed, desperate.

She smiled mischievously. "What do you think?" As the passerby drew closer, she draped her discarded cape over her head and shoulders and bent over his lap.

Her fingers curled around his cock.

She took its tip in her hot, wet mouth.

And Martin found himself suppressing his groan as the face of Mr. Sebright pulled into view.

"Good afternoon," he forced himself to say, raising a hand in a courtly wave.

Mr. Sebright bowed at the neck. "Good afternoon, Lord Preston. Have you been paying visits today?"

Mrs. Bellamy's tongue drew circles around Martin's shaft. He struggled to draw breath, much less come up with a proper answer. "No, I have been attending to business. And you?"

"I am on my way to see about some goats for the rectory," replied the reverend.

Martin didn't have the attention to notice whether the man was sanctimonious or earnest or solicitous. Mrs. Bellamy was now vigorously stimulating his cock with both her hands and her hot, hot mouth, taking it more deeply against her tongue than he would have thought possible. He exhaled loudly to keep from bucking his hips.

"Are you ill, sir?" asked Mr. Sebright.

"Headache," Martin managed to reply. "I had better get home."

"I wish you a speedy recovery."

The horses of both vehicles began to move again, and soon, Mr. Sebright was out of view. Mrs. Bellamy flicked her tongue across the tip of Martin's cock. A hand slipped down to fondle the soft skin of his balls. Martin had never felt so disintegrated, so fully tantalized, and he barely had time to sink back against the bench cushions before he exploded in one of the most intense orgasms of his life.

His whole body shook, every nerve crying out with pleasure, and his seed spurted endlessly into the hot back of Mrs. Bellamy's throat.

When at last he was spent, Mrs. Bellamy emerged from under her cape, smirking like the cat who ate the cream.

"That was dangerous," he scolded her, breathless. "We could have been discovered."

"But we weren't discovered, and now you have quite the memory of me to keep, haven't you?"

Martin found himself sliding off the bench to meet her on the floor of the carriage. He draped his arms—which still felt like wet noodles after his orgasm—around her and pulled her into a kiss. His heart was full of light peace, like the fluff of dandelion drifting in a summer breeze, and it was all because of her. He wanted to thank her; he wanted to hold her; he wanted to keep her by his side at all times.

He settled for promising her, "That's a memory I'll never forget," and held her in his arms until they reached Northfield once more.

MARTHA KNEW THIS WAS not Heaven. That was somewhere distant and unreachable, somewhere that the bliss of fulfilled lust could not touch. Yet, for this handful of weeks, she really did feel that she had been blessed by an angel, so happy was she.

Perhaps it was Kenneth, calling in favors beyond the pearly gates to bring her some peace after all these years. Perhaps it was merely the halo of Lord Preston with all his good deeds casting a little bit of its special glow upon her.

Whatever the cause, Martha did not dare question it. She floated along in this new river of joy: stolen kisses pressed to her knuckles when she handed Lord Preston a stack of correspondence to sign; ankles intertwining under the dining table where the footmen could not see; and best of all, after the household went to sleep, Lord Preston sneaking into her bedroom.

He never slept there the whole night, nor did they ever touch in view of anyone else. Still, Martha felt his eyes on her almost every moment they were in a room together—and if not his eyes, then his fingers, and if not his fingers, then his mouth.

She and Kenneth must have felt this way when they were newly married, in those heady first few months before they started worrying about a child, but it was too long ago for Martha to remember. This desire she felt towards Lord Preston, unadulterated with wifely concerns, seemed new and pure. He was nothing to her except a lover, and she did not owe him anything except her honest desire.

It was poisonously exciting.

On a day that he went to Thatcham to visit Mr. Maulvi, Martha remained behind—not wanting to risk running into old acquaintances who might notice her new cheer. She took her sewing basket down to the garden drawing room, where the wide windows let in plenty of natural light so she could see her stitches. She had to adjust her autumn clothes for mourning.

Conveniently, her seat in the drawing room also gave her a view of the painting above the mantel. This was a watercolor of Lady Preston with her five children. They looked out solemnly, yet one could feel the mother's love in how she draped one hand on a son's shoulder and held the littlest child—Caroline—in her lap.

Where had Lord Preston been when his family sat for this painting?

What did he see when he looked at it? Were all his memories rosy? Was there no woman who could compare with Lady Preston?

Martha was so absorbed that she was caught staring at the painting when Mrs. Chow entered, carrying a basket of books to be replaced on the shelf. Embarrassed, Martha greeted the other woman too brightly: "How goes your day, Mrs. Chow?"

The housekeeper looked a little surprised. Had Martha been cool to her up until now? Or had she simply been expecting to find the drawing room empty, assuming Martha had gone to Thatcham with Lord Preston? Mrs. Chow replied, "Fine, thank you. Do you need any refreshments?"

"No, thank you, though I would welcome your company, if you have a few moments to sit and rest."

Mrs. Chow considered the basket in her arms for a moment, then took Martha up on the offer. "My back aches so easily these days." The woman was around the same age as Martha, her hair a fine white that stood out nicely against the darker olive tone of her skin. She spoke English tilted by the accent of her native Chinese language, though the words came so easily that Martha hardly noticed it.

"Especially since you have grandchildren to race after," Martha said in sympathy. "Are you in great anticipation of Mr. Eddie Chow's child?"

Mrs. Chow waved her hand as if sweeping away bad luck. "A child is a blessing, that's what the English say, isn't it? Though they can run a mother's heart ragged, too."

Martha wasn't sure if Mrs. Chow meant to reference Lucas or if she meant it generally about any child, and so she kept her reply simple: "Yes."

"Eddie is my sweetest boy," Mrs. Chow went on, "but he gave me the greatest worry because of how he loved Miss Caroline. When they ran away together..."

Martha looked up to see the other woman shaking her head, her brow drawn with old heartache, and she considered that the story of Lucas might never have made it to the working people of Northfield Hall. Or, even if it had, Mrs. Chow might not remember that it belonged to Martha.

Or the woman still worried so deeply for Eddie, even though he and Caroline seemed happily settled, that she needed to hear a promise from Martha that he would not end his life the way Lucas had.

Martha folded her hands across her sewing. "My son eloped with an earl's daughter, and it ended in both their deaths. Hers of fever and his..." The grief that never went away surged upward. "He destroyed himself. I like to believe he thought that was the kindest way to end the ordeal, yet it only made things worse for me and his father, of course. Because we couldn't even—" But she would not cry. She had cried enough, and that wasn't the point she was trying to make. "We couldn't even give him a proper burial. I don't know if that is how you honor your dead, but for me, to not have a grave I can visit…Well, the heartache never ends."

Mrs. Chow watched her steadily. "I was furious with Eddie when he ran away with her. I did everything in my power to keep him from doing that, and then he went and did exactly what he should not have done. Were you furious?"

Martha surprised herself by laughing. She had forgotten, but *yes*, how angry she had been when they had first heard he was discovered in Bath with Lady Imogen! "Fury is not how a mother is supposed to express her love."

"But children are infuriating!"

"Oh, from the moment they are born," Martha agreed. "I remember the first time Lucas peed on me as I changed his nappy. Right in my eye! I thought, 'Now I'm supposed to give you a kiss? No, thank you!'" She wiped at her cheek as if to clear that old mess from her face. "Ah, but I would give anything to change his nappy again, if I could."

Mrs. Chow reached over and gave Martha's fingers a firm squeeze. "Your son was loved. That's what you must take comfort in."

"And your son *is* loved, by you and very much so by Caroline."

"*Very* much so," Mrs. Chow agreed, "and though I may never understand it, I do think it is strong enough for them to withstand life, so long as they have each other."

Which made Martha wonder: Had Lady Imogen survived her fever, would she and Lucas be living happily somewhere in Bath with a gaggle of children? Would Martha have been able to see them, or would she have been obliged to shun them to demonstrate proper moral fiber to Tolpuddle?

"In any case, once the baby is safely delivered, I shall be very happy and eager to love it. I find grandchildren far less infuriating than children. Now, if only Lord Preston would let Leyla replace me so I could retire to my cottage..."

The mention of her lover threatened to bring a blush to Martha's cheeks. She looked down at her sewing to keep her face from betraying anything. "Is he opposed to Leyla?" The head housemaid seemed more than competent to Martha's unaccustomed judgment.

"He is opposed to change. Just look at how he hasn't hired a new steward even though Mr. Maulvi has been ill the better part of the year." Mrs. Chow shook her head at the painting of Lady Preston and her children. "Ever since Caroline and Eddie ran off together, I think, he has not been willing to consider change unless it is forced upon him. But how can I force my retirement upon him? Aside from dying, which I really would rather not do."

Martha felt guilty at how excited she was to receive this glimpse of insight into Lord Preston. She ran her finger over the seam she had just finished. "He is hoping Lord Benjamin will become the steward."

Mrs. Chow said, "And secretary, too? You are kind to help him in the meantime, but he must make plans to hire someone permanently, mustn't he?"

He would hire someone, of course, and Martha would eventually go live with her niece. But she didn't want to think about that. Measuring her delivery so as not to sound too eager, she said, "Perhaps I could broach the subject with him. Not overtly, of course, but to begin to suggest to him that you are deserving of your idle days now."

Mrs. Chow looked at Martha for a beat too long before saying, "Yes, if you feel comfortable saying something like that, it is worth a try." Then, looking back at the family portrait, she added, "You remind me of Lady Preston a little, you know. You are very steady in yourself."

Was she? Martha more often felt as if she were calling on every reserve to stay steady against life's headwinds. Such as now, when she should not ask—should not fan the flames of Mrs. Chow's suspicions—and yet did: "What was Lady Preston like?"

"Very stubborn. Which was good when I agreed with her and bad when I didn't." Mrs. Chow smiled. "She was very dedicated to whatever she decided to do, and like Lord Preston, she had very strong ideas of what it was a person was *supposed* to do. She loved her children, of course, and she and Lord Preston were very much in love. Did you know her father disowned her for marrying him?"

Martha hadn't known that. "Was she of such high birth that marrying Lord Preston was a step down?"

"No, but he hired Mr. Chow and me. He might as well have hosted an orgy, if you asked Lady Preston's father, for it made Lord Preston a dangerous renegade."

"That's terrible."

Mrs. Chow shrugged. "That is life."

Martha's imagination floated away, painting Lord Preston's marriage with the brush of star-crossed love. No wonder he was so devoted to Lady Preston if they had overcome so much in order to marry! "Is it true that he has never courted another woman since her death?"

"None that I have heard of," Mrs. Chow said, "and everyone seems to want to tell me when they hear something scandalous about the family." She pinned Martha under her gaze. "It has been fifteen years, though. If he finds happiness with someone else, I say it's high time."

She would *not* smile, nor would she blush, nor would she confess the cacophony of feelings she had about Lord Preston, even though she felt certain Mrs. Chow would not judge her for their indecorous behavior. "Friendships come and go in life. Perhaps he does not need to find final happiness with someone else to enjoy some companionship while sharing a path."

Mrs. Chow nodded. "That too. Happiness is happiness, isn't it?"

"Yes." Although it did come in a million variations. Right now, Martha's happiness from feeling understood by a new friend was hemmed in by her whirling questions about Lord Preston. Was she happy, or was she excited, or was she about to fall apart at the seams if she heard the wrong answer to her questions? She put on a smile for Mrs. Chow. "I am so grateful to have been welcomed at Northfield Hall while I make arrangements with my family."

"We are glad to have you." Mrs. Chow rose from the settee with a few creaks. "Now, I had better get back to work before Leyla thinks I keeled over. If you need help with that mending, let me know. Renee is a wonderful seamstress."

"Thank you, but I like to have something to do." Martha wished she had something more valuable to say—or something more sincere to express the feeling of friendship blossoming in her heart. She settled for "I have enjoyed your company."

"People usually do," Mrs. Chow quipped, and she exited with her basket.

Chapter Eleven

MAULVI WAS SOUNDING BETTER but looking worse. Every time Martin visited, the other man seemed to have shrunk, his skin looking duller and duller against the fresh linens that the Widow Croft changed every morning. His face was almost all cheekbones now, without any fat to round out the smile that had greeted Martin all his life.

Smile he did, though, at Martin's appearance, and his voice sounded as strong as ever when he said, "At last you have returned. I thought you must have replaced me already and forgotten all about me."

"There is no replacing you." Martin sank into the wooden chair upholstered in leather that Lolly had gifted Widow Croft's household some decades ago. The sentiment was true: Maulvi had been a servant of Martin's family since before Martin was born, and losing him was going to hurt Martin more deeply than losing his own father.

"You must replace me," Maulvi said, the smile dimming, "for I know what happens if you are without a supervisor. You'll decide we should grow peat."

"That was *one* idea—and when I was all of twelve, I might add."

"That you brought up again when you wanted to do away with our coal purchases."

Martin allowed the man his ribbing. It was good to see him cheerful.

Maulvi asked, "Have you solved the problem of the cottages for the Beauchamps?"

Ah, but that was why they had rubbed along together so well all these years: at heart, they were both workhorses. "The problem of the cottages is a problem of physics as well as a problem of resources."

"In other words, your pockets are too empty to do anything about it."

Not empty. But Martin didn't want to explain to Maulvi the dilemma of spending the small reserves of his bank account on purchasing new land versus leaving a financial legacy for his children. It was too depressing—and, unlike Mrs. Bellamy, Maulvi had too much of an interest in the children to comfort Martin that he was doing his best.

If this was his best, then Martin was neither a very good father nor a very good baron.

"Aren't you supposed to be retired from such concerns? I hope you haven't been spending your days reading old estate reports.

Surely there must be something more interesting to occupy your thoughts."

"Oh, I don't need to read an estate report to know exactly what is going on. The wheat is drying too slowly because of the cold; the women's dormitory is full to capacity; and Jarvoise is still complaining that you haven't given him enough budget to properly care for the azaleas."

Martin admitted to each guess being true.

"*And—*" Maulvi continued, "you have put poor Mrs. Bellamy to work because you cannot bring yourself to hire a steward to replace me."

The room suddenly felt too hot. "She *wanted* the work. She said she would be at loose ends without something to occupy her."

"Are you now a man with a secretary, then? Have you hired the widow on a permanent basis?"

Martin could not look his friend in the eye. "No, she is only helping until she hears from her niece."

He had been spending an inordinate amount of time considering the errant letter from the niece, name unknown. When it arrived, would Mrs. Bellamy pack her things and leave within the day? What if her niece said there was only room for her to sleep on a pallet in the room with the children, like a nursemaid? Could Mrs. Bellamy hope to be happy as a hanger-on to a family member who she hadn't seen for over a decade?

Of course, she must be. It was the proper and natural course of action for a person to spend their last years with their remaining family. As much as he and Mrs. Bellamy enjoyed each other's company now—and he was aware that even in his own thoughts, he avoided naming the fire that erupted between their bodies—she could not be happy living for long in his shadow at Northfield Hall. She deserved to be in a home where she had a proper place, and where she never had to question how long she was welcome.

Maulvi peered at Martin as the Widow Croft served them each a cup of chamomile-and-ginger tisane. When she had bustled back into the kitchen, Maulvi asked, "I don't know Mrs. Bellamy well. What is she like?"

Martin made a meal out of sipping his drink so he could think of a proper answer. "She is made of strong stuff. No matter what circumstance she is presented with, she will find a way to tolerate it."

"Is she in deep grief over the loss of her husband?"

His tisane spilled onto his knee. Martin jerked up at the shock of hot liquid. Cursing, he did his best to clean it up with his handkerchief.

Maulvi waited for the commotion to end before prompting, "You were going to tell me more about Mrs. Bellamy."

Martin should change the subject. Maulvi knew him too well, and Martin was too full of thoughts about Mrs. Bellamy to keep them secret.

Thoughts—and feelings.

"What is there to tell? I do not know how she feels about her late husband. She is intelligent, well informed, kind, discerning. Her handwriting is elegant. What else could there be to say?"

"Is she good company?"

Martin forced himself to behave like a normal, civilized human being. "Yes."

Maulvi watched him, and he watched Maulvi, and Martin found himself admitting:

"She has seduced me."

To his credit, Maulvi did not guffaw, though his eyebrows did jump to the top of his brow. "*She* has seduced *you*?"

"Well, I didn't intend to act on my...inclinations, if you see what I mean, but she persuaded me it would not hurt either of us."

"And?"

And Martin wasn't sure if it was true that neither of them would be hurt. When he was in the same room as Mrs. Bellamy, he was intoxicated by her, but when apart from her, he filled with a sense of foreboding.

They did not belong together. Their time together would end. And when it did, how could that ending be anything but hurtful?

"Has it only happened the one time?" Maulvi asked.

Martin felt his cheeks flame with shame. It *should* have been limited to the one time, shouldn't it? He had indulged himself and Mrs. Bellamy, and when he had returned to his senses, he should have resolved not to let it happen again.

"Then perhaps she has done more than seduce you," Maulvi said into Martin's silence. "Have you fallen in love?"

At this, Martin could honestly scoff. "It has been hardly a month, Maulvi. I find her interesting and pleasing and..." *Intoxicating*, but he would not say that aloud. "Yet I hardly know her well enough to consider myself in love with her."

"I do not recall that it took you so long to declare your love to Lady Preston."

But he had already been engaged to Lolly before he fell in love with her. Even if they had not anticipated an actual wedding, Martin had had every right to fall in love with Lolly. And besides, he had been young and his idea of love had been simple.

Having loved Lolly for twenty ensuing years, Martin could look back and see that what he had considered love before their wedding had merely been the seeds necessary to grow into deep, layered, intense love.

Perhaps—perhaps!—a few of those seeds were germinating between him and Mrs. Bellamy. But Martin knew better than to give them any light or water.

She was not for him.

"Lolly was Lolly," Martin replied. "Come now, old man, surely we do not want to turn into boring gossips. What do you think I should do about the wheat?"

Maulvi frowned at him. "It is not gossip if it is your own heart at stake, sir."

"My heart is safe and sound," Martin promised. "Now, have we put enough food stores away that I need not worry about a bad crop?"

Maulvi let the topic drop. But when the Widow Croft came in to tell Martin he had visited long enough, the old man asked his common-law wife, "Is it possible to have two loves of your life, do you think, dear Rebecca?"

She grinned at him. "Sure I do, for I had Mr. Croft and now these last forty years, I've been blessed with you."

Maulvi looked at Martin as if he had won an argument. But Martin's concern was not that it was impossible for him to love again; he knew only that it couldn't be with Mrs. Bellamy.

As September bled into October, evening came sooner and sooner—and Martha grew ever more eager to retire to her bedroom, where she could wait for Lord Preston's knock. She made a ritual of changing into her dressing robe, brushing out her hair with a hundred strokes, and dabbing on perfume from her dwindling supply. She always had time to remove her stockings to greet him with bare feet on the hardwood floor, but he never kept her waiting long enough for her to light the candles beside her bed.

That they did together, sometime after their first kiss by the door and their four-footed steps to the mattress.

He loved her long hair. Some nights—usually after their first bout of lovemaking—he sat her up and ran his fingers through her hair as if they were the brush. "It's terribly thin compared to what it used to be," Martha said self-consciously on one of their first nights together, and Lord Preston objected, "It is beautiful as it is. So silver, like Rumpelstiltskin himself spun it!"

She had never thought of it that way, so she let him keep on admiring it.

He loved her hands, too. Almost always, he greeted her first by bringing one hand at a time to his lips and kissing each fingertip, his eyes locked on hers. It made her feel like a queen. Once, she curtsied—and he pulled her to her feet and thrust his tongue inside of her right there beside her closed bedroom door.

When the full moon came, they left the candles unlit and tied back the curtains so the room flooded with moonlight. Hidden in the shadows—knowing he couldn't see her drooping breasts or sagging stomach—Martha climbed atop Lord Preston and rode him as if she were a twenty-year-old harlot. She even placed his thumb on her nub, earning herself the loudest orgasm of her life.

"You'll wake the household," he said as she spilled into his arms in the aftermath, but there was a smile in his voice instead of a scold.

"You have turned me into a lusty creature," she replied, taking his earlobe in her lips to drive him a little crazy.

"*I* have turned *you* into a lusty creature? My dear Mrs. Bellamy, you are the one who demanded I consider your point of view." He emphasized this by pulling her closer against his body.

She wanted him to call her Martha, but she hadn't yet found the courage to ask for it. It was such an intimate gesture, far more significant than finding mutual pleasure in each other's bodies.

If he began calling her Martha, it suggested she expected they would always be in a position for him to be so familiar. And on the other hand, if she asked him to call her Martha and he declined, she would hardly be able to face him again.

She wished she had an in-between name, like he did with Preston, but she was not a woman blessed with honorary titles and Christian names that stretched on for days. Another reason she didn't want to bring it up: perhaps the courtly ladies of London did not ask their lovers to use their first names, and Martha's request would only serve to remind him of all the ways she did not fit into his world.

She pacified herself by kissing him deeply for a little while. With one hand fastening her hip in place against his groin, he threaded fingers through her hair. They were spent and tired, so this kissing would lead to nothing but the warm feeling that had her sleeping through the nights.

Eventually, however, even the kissing came to an end, and this time, Lord Preston withdrew, nestling his cheek on the pillow close—but not close enough—to her face. "The cold is going to come before we know it."

She snaked her feet between his. "We can keep each other warm."

"Yes." Smiling, he pushed some errant hairs from her brow. His hand rested on her neck in a lazy, possessive curl. "But I am a little worried about your travels. Wouldn't it be better to arrive at your niece's before winter makes the roads dangerous?"

They had not mentioned such practical things in weeks. Martha rolled onto her back, looking to the canopy above her bed for the right reply. "Her name is Georgina."

He withdrew his hand. "Do you think you should write to Georgina again? Perhaps your last note got lost in the mail."

Though the possibility had occurred to Martha, too, she did not want to admit to the necessity of writing again. "It is not a simple thing to take in another family member. You may forget what it is like for us common folk, but our houses are not made of endless rooms and the hearths aren't filled with coal. Taking me in might mean the family goes hungry this winter."

"Yet family has a duty to care for each other, even when it is difficult. You deserve to be welcomed by your family."

Tears threatened. Martha shut her eyes and indulged herself in a deep, silent breath.

Lord Preston added, "I only want what is best for you. If it is a question of money, then I could settle something upon you—"

Martha kept her eyes closed as she cut him off: "Like a discarded mistress?"

The comment was too sharp. Martha felt consumed by the word *mistress*—a brazen woman, a stupid woman, a heinous woman. She didn't notice Lord Preston roll away until she had banished her tears and discovered their bodies no longer touched at all.

On his stomach, staring down at his pillow, he said stiffly, "I did not mean to imply such a thing."

But he didn't need to *imply,* because the truth was, the only thing distinguishing Martha from a mistress was the matter of money. "And I don't mean to be ungrateful in the face of your generosity. I wish to cleave our actions from financial matters. You are not in my bed because I want your money. Nor am I in your bed so you may control me with the promise of it."

"I do not want to control you. I want to do right by you." These last words barely came out as he slammed his fists into the pillow. Martha startled backward on the mattress. "I'll stop trying," he growled. "All I manage to do is fail."

"You have hardly *failed.* We are only having a conversation."

"I have failed enough people to know when I am about to fail another."

Which was when Martha recognized his emotions: they were the same ones that had sent him careening to the mantelpiece when Caroline had deserted their Sunday dinner. She reached out to rest her palm on his bare back. "I am not dependent upon you, Preston. I have money to take rooms at an inn until I hear from Georgina, and if I never hear from her, then I shall take in mending and make do. So you see, you cannot fail me, because I am not asking for anything from you."

He turned his head on the pillow to look at her. "I made you feel indecent."

"You have many powers in this land, sir, but even you cannot control how I feel." She had managed to make herself feel indecent all on her own.

For a moment, he was silent—though he turned on his side to mirror her, and his hand found hers as her palm slid from his back to his hip. "Still, you were upset, and it is because of what I said."

"It is because you reminded me of a reality I do not want to face."

"That was the last thing I wanted to do."

She did not believe him: he *had* wanted her to consider the practical question of Georgina, or else he would not have introduced it. But she did believe that he had not wanted to bring tears to her eyes. "I forgive you."

Holding hands, they inhaled and exhaled together.

Soon would come the next ritual of the evening: his departure. Martha would walk him to the door for one last kiss, and she would leave it cracked, just in case he wanted to slip back in. She would brush her hair again and braid it in two plaits. She would wash her face, her armpits, her happily exercised muff, and she would wrap herself in their blankets and sleep until sunrise.

But she didn't have to go through that yet. He was still in bed with her, and Martha could lean forward to claim another kiss. Which she did. It tasted all the sweeter for having survived their argument.

"I've never known a person like you before," he said, holding tight to her fingers.

"What, a lusty old widow?"

His smile carved a dark line in the dark room. "A person whose kindness is honesty. You make everything seem clearer and simpler."

"Not simple, just not quite as complicated as you make it."

Tugging her close, he said, "Whatever happens in the end, I am so grateful to have you as my friend, Mrs. Bellamy."

She didn't like his talk of the end. She didn't like being called a friend, even though it was her own term to replace *mistress* or *courtesan* or whatever else a person might rightfully call her.

But for whatever reason, she only made one objection: "Don't you think it is about time we leave Kenneth out of it and you call me Martha instead?"

"Martha." He drew it out so it sounded like a poem. He kissed her fingertips, making her a queen. "I am so glad to know you, Martha."

"Yes. You should be." And, before he left, they laughed together again.

Chapter Twelve

The inevitable news arrived by a farmhand who raced on a horse to tell Northfield: Mr. Maulvi had died.

Martin had known this was coming. Maulvi was fifteen years older than him and in declining health, and the Widow Croft had been keeping their visits shorter and shorter because Maulvi got tired from even the easiest conversation.

The news stole his breath nonetheless. The farmhand delivered it from the threshold of the study while Martin sat at his desk, reviewing a potential contract for the eastern farm, and Martin had to put his forehead to the paper to keep from being overwhelmed.

Maulvi. The man who had guided Martin since he was a child. Who had spoken honestly when Martin's ideas had gotten ahead of him. Who had overseen every little detail of the Northfield estate while Martin envisioned grand change.

Who had been kind, funny, firm, caring—who had single-handedly kept Martin rising from his bed after Lolly died.

Maulvi was gone.

Mrs. Bellamy, who had been at work on a letter to the London housekeeper about repairs to a broken step, thanked the farmhand and draped her arm around Martin's shoulders. She didn't say anything. Didn't ask anything of him, didn't weep herself, didn't do anything except keep her body close to his.

Martin had the urge to go ask Maulvi what would happen if he fell in love with her.

But Maulvi had died in the night, his breath rattling on no more, and any wisdom he had for Martin had evaporated with that last exhalation.

And how selfish was Martin to *need* something of Maulvi even in his death? Just one more way that he had failed his old friend. If he even had the right to call him a friend.

He pulled himself together, reining in first his thoughts, then his spine, and finally shrugging off Mrs. Bellamy's hand. "I must go to the Widow Croft," he said, straightening his papers. "There is much to arrange."

"I'll go with you."

"You needn't come—"

She interrupted firmly, "I am going for Becky Croft, not for you, sir."

Which reminded Martin of how he had failed Mrs. Bellamy, too: already, he had reduced her in his mind to a fantastic creature made for his loving and forgotten that she was a woman in her own right. A woman who had in her lifetime, no doubt, comforted a hundred widows at their husbands' deathbeds.

He was being self-indulgent. Shaking off his thoughts, he focused on tasks instead of judgments: ordering the carriage readied, changing into boots, giving instructions for six men to begin digging a grave in the family plot. Mrs. Bellamy wore her cape as she climbed into the carriage with a hamper of food. At the last minute, Martin called for his cloak, though it delayed them by nearly a quarter hour.

Widow Croft's home was abuzz with activity when they arrived. Someone had already draped the windows with black bombazine; two women and a boy sloshed a tub of water into the street as Martin helped Mrs. Bellamy from the carriage. When they reached the upstairs bedroom, Widow Croft sat by the bed, where the body was wrapped in a white linen shroud.

Everyone quieted when Martin entered. He crossed to Widow Croft, knelt beside her, and took her spare hand. "He was the dearest man alive to me. The world is the poorer for losing him."

"And you were the dearest man alive to him," she replied. Martin was surprised by how she could smile—not a tear in her eye!

Even though Lolly's death had been long coming, too, Martin had shattered when finally she was gone. Widow Croft seemed in almost the same mood as during his visit the week before.

Was he weak for being so crushed when those around him died? Or was Widow Croft more unfeeling?

He shouldn't judge, not at a time like this. Standing, he waited for Mrs. Bellamy to make her remarks to the widow before introducing the topic of arrangements. Maulvi had discussed his requests with both Martin and Widow Croft, so they knew exactly what he wanted: to be buried as soon as possible in the family plot at Northfield, beside his parents, turned on his right side and with his head pointing to the east—towards Mecca.

"That sweet Mr. Zaman has already washed him and said the special prayer," Widow Croft reported. "Oh, I hope you won't tell Mr. Sebright, Mrs. Bellamy, though of course I'm already out of favor with the church for being a common-law wife all these years."

"That is between you and your conscience, and I tend to think the Lord must make allowances for situations like these," said Mrs. Bellamy kindly.

Rising, Martin asked as delicately as he could, "Would you like to ride in the carriage with us as we take the body to Northfield? I have men readying the grave so that we may honor dear Maulvi's request for immediate burial."

"It is the custom of his people, and he never wanted to turn his back on them," Widow Croft explained to Mrs. Bellamy. To Martin, she replied, "For myself, I'm an Englishwoman through and through, and it's not for me to be at the graveside."

Her voice wavered a little with emotion. Martin took her hand again. "You may count on us to do our duty by Maulvi."

She looked at the shrouded body. "He said the best way to honor him was with acts of charity in his name. We agreed I would host an assembly in a month's time to raise funds for the Lascars. My Maulvi was always reading about the plight of those poor fellows. I think that will be a nice way to say farewell, don't you, sir?"

It was certainly a singular way to say farewell. Martin was saved from finding a reply by Caroline's arrival.

Martin hadn't seen her for a few weeks, and he was startled by how much larger she had grown, the baby making itself known even under the loose drape of her dress. She rushed to the widow and pulled her into a warm embrace. "Aunt Croft, I don't know what we'll do without Uncle Maulvi."

"He is out of his pain at last," the widow replied, patting Caroline's back fondly. "I take consolation in knowing that he is free of mortal burdens. Perhaps he is even now learning the answers to the eternal questions that always intrigued him."

"Oh yes, or at the very least, I hope he is finding out whether pigs really do ever fly." Withdrawing from the embrace, Caroline turned to Martin. "Papa, it is so sad."

"Uncle Maulvi loved you very much," he said, hoping they were the right words.

Her eyes shone bright with tears. "He always knew exactly the right advice to give, didn't he?"

"He took great joy in being a mentor to you and your siblings."

She nodded, frustration sneaking into her expression, though Martin couldn't imagine why. Was he not agreeing with everything she said? And was this not Maulvi's deathbed—couldn't the man have peace from Preston dramatics *now*, if not in life?

"And you loved him," Caroline prompted.

"Yes." Martin looked at the sheet covering the body of the man who was his closest friend. "I am glad to have been able to visit him since returning from London. We had some good final conversations."

He discovered he wasn't quite able to get the words out, for they provoked a terrible wave of sadness that closed his throat. Instinctively, he turned away. Mrs. Bellamy touched his elbow. "Mr. Maulvi meant the world to his lordship."

Her fingers seared through his jacket. Of course, Martin wanted to lean into her arms, but the gesture—the words implying she had private knowledge of his feelings—made his heart stutter with horror. She might as well have tried to kiss him right there in front of Caroline and the Widow Croft.

He withdrew from her touch. Summoning centuries of decorum, he returned to practicalities: "Caroline, would you please write to inform your siblings? Mrs. Croft will host an assembly to honor Mr. Maulvi in a month's time, and she hopes they may join us there."

His daughter looked at him with some new, terrible emotion in her eyes. Horror, no doubt. He did not concern himself about it. That had always been Maulvi's advice: *let them* feel what they were going to feel, whether *they* were his grown children or the peers of the realm. So long as Martin was honest and true, he could not worry about the judgment of those who did not understand him.

And, his affair with Mrs. Bellamy excepted, he remained honest and true.

"Yes, Papa," Caroline said, "but first I shall sit with Aunt Croft for a while."

"Fine." Martin suddenly couldn't stand to be in that room full of women—women, and Maulvi's body. "I shall find some men to move the...to move...Mrs. Bellamy, will you return to Northfield in the carriage?"

She should not come, not after that display, yet he could not help hoping she would say, "Yes, indeed, I must return with you." Otherwise, he would be alone in the carriage with Maulvi's body. He might forget that *he* was still alive.

But Mrs. Bellamy had good sense. She had stepped away from him already, and she did not even look at him as she replied, "No, sir, I'll stay here with Mrs. Croft."

Which meant Martin had no choice:

He left her behind.

MARTHA DID NOT LIKE how Lord Preston took his leave. She did not like the way he jerked away from her touch as if her fingers were hot irons; she did not like how he and Caroline had almost erupted into another argument; and most of all, she did not like being left behind at Mrs. Croft's.

It was her duty to be there—as much in her role as Kenneth's late wife as in her own right as a community member. When a person died, Martha was one of the people who swooped in to keep their household running through their grief.

But she did not actually know Mrs. Croft well, and the room was already full of people seeing to her needs far better than Martha could. The farm women who had emptied the tub returned, and they took charge of cleaning the room and serving everyone tea. The boy, a nephew of Mrs. Croft, offered scones before scarfing them down himself. Caroline took the place of honor, pulling up a stool beside Mrs. Croft and sharing stories about "Uncle Maulvi."

Knowing Lord Preston as she did now, Martha couldn't help but find surprising the familiarity between Caroline and Mrs. Croft, the latter of whom spoke with a loose Berkshire accent and likely couldn't name a member of the peerage outside the Preston family. Martha had previously assumed that this was a result of Lord Preston's desire to break down all invisible barriers between men; but she had discovered these past two months that, in fact, he stood on ceremony more often than not.

Such as when he took his leave so awkwardly, backing away from her as if being in proximity to her would stain his reputation.

How, then, had he raised his daughter to call his steward Uncle and to marry below her station? Had Lady Preston been the radical class breaker? Or did it have nothing to do with the parents and everything to do with Caroline as an original?

Retreating to the little kitchen where a batch of bread dough sat rising in a bowl, Martha did her best to make herself useful, tidying up here and there. She hadn't any right to go back with Lord Preston anyhow. The burial was, as Mrs. Croft had said, the man's sphere.

Martha had once understood the custom that kept women away from the graveside. She hadn't wanted to see her father closed up in a coffin, nor did she think she could bear to watch it lowered into the hole. In fact, she had nightmares about graves that had no bottom, whose darkness went on and on through layers of dirt and tree roots and rock so that the coffin fell directly into Hell, with no chance of redemption.

If she had those fears without ever seeing a burial, she used to reason, it was a good idea to keep her and all other tender-hearted women from seeing what actually happened.

Then Lucas died. Or *destroyed himself*, as the inquest described it. *Murdered himself*, as one of the Bath newspapers reported.

Of all the bodies to avoid, Martha knew it should be his: because he was her son, because he had done something terrible, and because through the act of shooting himself in the head, he had made his body a hellish monster. Yet, when Kenneth told her what Lucas had done, she had been consumed with a need to hold her son one last time. Whatever was left of him. She wanted to hug him. She wanted to bathe him. She wanted to dress him in his final clothes and be the last one to touch him before he descended into the cold grave.

She was his mother. She should have had that right.

Of course, even if anyone would have allowed it, she didn't get the chance. By the time she and Kenneth got the news, Lucas had already been buried at the crossroads.

Martha had done her best to remain a good rector's wife, and so she did not beg to attend any burials. When they moved to

Thatcham, however, she discovered she could stand just behind the rectory's henhouse for a view down onto the parish cemetery. On burial days, she wrapped herself in her black mourning shawl and stood in her spot, imagining that each coffin was Lucas's coffin, that each mourner was someone who loved her son offering him forgiveness as he descended to his final resting spot.

It never quite gave her *comfort*, but it didn't make her feel worse, either. When Kenneth died, she had slipped out—despite hosting a dozen women in the parish house that very moment—and imagined him falling through a bottomless grave to find Lucas. Kenneth was a good man who had done his best; he deserved to go to Heaven, but Martha secretly hoped he had gone to keep their son company until she could join them.

If only she could have accepted Lord Preston's invitation to attend Mr. Maulvi's burial. To stand by a graveside as it happened—to smell the freshly dug dirt and see the sweat on the gravediggers' brows—Martha yearned to know every detail so that she could pretend she had been at Lucas's burial. But if Mrs. Croft didn't want to go, then Martha certainly wasn't going to. She knew death well enough to know that her duty—any woman's duty—was to the living.

Hearing Mrs. Croft and the others emerge into the common room from the bedroom where Mr. Maulvi had expired, Martha gave herself a stern shake and rejoined the group. Caroline sat beside Mrs. Croft on the worn sofa while everyone listened to the boy recite the multiplication table. When he got to "Ten by ten equals one hundred," Mrs. Croft broke into applause. "Ah, how proud Mr. Maulvi is—was—of you, Billy!"

Martha didn't belong to this group of people who knew each other so well. She forced herself to claim the other side of the sofa anyway. It wasn't as if she had anywhere to go.

"It's very kind of you to comfort me, Mrs. Bellamy," said Mrs. Croft, "especially as you are still in the midst of your own mourning."

"I did not know Mr. Maulvi well, but I was always glad to meet him."

"And he you, I'm sure. He told me after Lord Preston's last visit that he was glad you are at Northfield Hall to be a friend to his lordship." Mrs. Croft said this without any malice, yet even Martha was struck by how strange a sentiment it was for Mr. Maulvi to have shared.

She feared what Lord Preston might have said to him about their friendship.

On the other side of Mrs. Croft, Caroline lifted an eyebrow.

"I am grateful I can be of use to his lordship while I wait for word from my family." The words scraped a little against her soul as she said them, since in fact she *didn't* want to hear from Georgina, but Martha had long since learned how to say the right thing instead of the true thing. And in this case, the right thing was anything that might quell rumors. "Mr. Bellamy always said my penmanship was good enough to be a secretary's, and I am glad to prove him right."

"Our lost ones remain with us in those ways," Mrs. Croft said with a sad little nod.

"I think your idea of a charity ball in Mr. Maulvi's honor is wonderful. Will you tell me how I can help?"

"Oh, Mrs. Chow here has offered to do most of it." Mrs. Croft patted Caroline's hand. "You must let Mrs. Bellamy assist, as well as anyone else who offers. It is their way of sharing their grief."

Caroline accepted this advice with a placid smile. What she said next, however, sent icy foreboding down Martha's spine: "I know exactly where to find you, Mrs. Bellamy, so expect that I shall visit my father soon with ideas of how you might help."

CHAPTER THIRTEEN

A STRANGE BUSINESS IT was, putting one's friend in the ground. Maulvi's religion called for no coffin, only a white shroud, and so Martin watched the shape of the body descend into its hole. He had to resist the urge to rush forward and peel the cloth from Maulvi's face to confirm his friend hadn't resumed breathing. A crowd of men from Northfield gathered to pay their respects; a Bengali weaver led them in prayer as they each tossed in three handfuls of dirt. When the gravediggers—groundskeepers who themselves wept as they saw to their task—started piling the freshly dug dirt back in, Martin looked at the markers of Maulvi's parents for comfort. Soon, his friend's grave would be covered in soft grass like theirs, adorned with flowers that Widow Croft or Mrs. Chow or he himself placed.

He wished he could cry. He had cried at Lolly's graveside, and it had been a great release of grief that let him survive the following days. But Maulvi's burial was something of a shock: he had only just died! There had been no service, no wake, none of the customs to which Martin was accustomed. His tears weren't ready yet.

He remained at the graveside as long as it took them to fill it up, which was to say hours. When he grew chilly, he took a shovel from one of the younger men and threw in dirt until his back protested. A soft, gentle rain began to fall, one that didn't soak his wool cloak but collected on his eyelashes like tears, and Martin was glad that at least whoever controlled the heavens above felt the same as him in this moment.

At last, the grave was full—and Maulvi gone.

Martin was moved to say a silent, final prayer, one that came from his heart instead of a book: *Let him live in joy for eternity.*

He walked back to Northfield Hall alone. He had remained in the soft rain long enough that his cloak was at last wet and rivulets dropped from the rim of his hat onto the back of his neck. His boots were a muddy mess. When he entered the side door, he took them off immediately and proceeded down the back corridor in damp stockinged feet.

Strange, how one was expected to go on living when the people you loved disappeared from the world.

He was halfway up the stairs when he heard Mrs. Bellamy from below: "There you are!"

She stood in the threshold between the foyer and the study, her hand on the doorknob as if ready to pull it shut at his direction. Her silver hair caught the candlelight and made it hover, almost like a halo.

Martin's heart surged into his throat in relief at seeing her.

"I made a plate of food for you. It's in here if you want it." She beckoned him to the study.

"My clothes are wet," he said stupidly.

Mrs. Bellamy's hand twisted the doorknob. "I could bring it up to your rooms, if you prefer?"

Martin knew two things: he wanted to be with her, and he couldn't bear to invite her into Lolly's bedroom. He descended the steps. "It's mostly my stockings. If it won't offend you, I'll hang them to dry by the fire in the study instead."

She rewarded him with a soft smile. "It won't offend me."

The tray of food waited on the table by the hearth, but Martin wasn't hungry. When the door latched behind them, he entwined his fingers through hers. Human touch—but it was more than that. She was no mere human; she was Martha, a friend like no other he had ever known. She didn't need him to say in words the bewildered loss that waited to swallow him whole. She sat him down on the sofa where they had first made love and unrolled his stockings one at a time. Hanging them on the elegant metal screen protecting the room from leaping embers, she selected a blanket from a nearby chair and draped it over his lap and around his bare ankles.

He had not earned such kindness from her. "I didn't want to leave you behind at Widow Croft's."

Mrs. Bellamy shook her head. "It was the proper thing to do."

"What is proper is not always right."

"And there isn't always right or wrong. There's just whatever happens. It has been a difficult day. Let us set it aside." She sat with him at last, having finished fussing over him. Martin wrapped his arm around her shoulders so that she snuggled against his chest, her head resting just below his chin.

It was not a surprise that his body had been so eager to enjoy hers these past weeks. He was, after all, still a man, and a man who had been denying his carnal needs for over a decade at that. What he didn't like to admit to himself was how much he craved the moments when he held her close without any eroticism at all. These were the embraces he had cherished with Lolly; he hadn't realized he could find them with someone else.

"Do you grieve your husband?" he asked, a question he should perhaps have asked a long time before.

"Of course. He was my partner for forty years. Even if I had hated the man, I'm sure I would grieve him in some way. One grieves what one is accustomed to."

"But you didn't hate him."

"No. I loved him." Her fingers ran along the edge of her hair, a nervous habit. "Our love was not soul-consuming. I am not heart-broken. But in losing him, I lost the person who knew me best, along with all that held my life together. To lose a husband is to lose everything."

"And to lose a wife is only to lose your heart."

She settled her palm on his chest. "Lucas certainly felt that was the same as losing everything."

"I suppose you have things you wish you could say to him."

"Oh, yes." She burrowed her cheek a little further into his rumpled cravat. "Things I wish I could say to him now. Things I wish I could have said to stop him from taking his life. Things I wish I could have said to keep the whole tragedy from happening. But he didn't listen to us when we warned him off Lady Imogen. Why would he have listened to me had I promised him I would forgive him no matter what?"

Martin remembered the terror that had seized him when Lady Charlotte informed him that Caroline had vanished with Eddie into the London night—and how that terror had transformed him into a desperate, furious man. If she had not come back alive...but even now, Martin couldn't contemplate that possibility. He asked Mrs. Bellamy, "Have you forgiven him?"

She tightened her hold on him. "Most days. Some days, I am furious with him all over again for taking his life. He should have come home, no matter the consequences."

"He forgot his duty to you," Martin said, trying to comfort her.

She broke into a choked sob. "I failed him, that's what it is at the end of the day, and I can never make it right."

Martin knew all too well what it was to fail the people one wanted most to help. He held Martha close, kissing her hair every now and then, and counted his failures as the fire leapt around the coals in the hearth. Caroline and Eddie, who had deserved his support. The Widow Croft, who he judged instead of supported. Maulvi, whom he had for too long treated as a servant while calling him a friend.

Oh, how he would miss his friend Maulvi. The tears he had waited for at last came, on a wave of grief as pure as it was intense, and Martin let them fall, though they dripped from his chin onto Martha's silver hair. She turned her head to look up at him, revealing wet eyes of her own, and placed a warm hand on his cheek. He mimicked her, holding her soft and strong cheek in his palm, and they stayed in that strange embrace for as long as they needed to let the day end.

THE BEAUTIFUL PART OF death, in Martha's mind, was how it brought out the kindness in everyone nearby. Those who didn't say more than "good day" to one on a regular day stopped to express their sympathy; a pantry that ordinarily stood embarrassingly empty filled with gifts from households all around; a lonely parlor filled with visitors. At Northfield Hall, Mr. Maulvi was celebrated with a beautiful outpouring of grief as every man, woman, and child paused to remember him. They left notes of remembrance in his office until his desktop couldn't be seen for all the little papers adorning it. When the rain cleared a day or so after the burial, they lit a bonfire and spent an evening raising drinks to anecdotes of Mr. Maulvi. A group of children recited a poem in his memory.

Martha learned that Mr. Maulvi had been kind to newcomers yet firm about estate rules. He had prioritized safety over production, and he had always been happy to see family members reunited.

Lord Preston featured in many of the anecdotes shared. He dipped his chin whenever his name came up, and Martha could read from that expression that he wanted to duck away but held himself to a standard that required him to bear the story manfully. Invariably, he was the hero—or accessory to the hero—of each anecdote: a lord so benevolent, so generous, so selfless that he put all men around him except Mr. Maulvi to shame.

She had heard stories like these a dozen times during her life in Thatcham. Everyone lauded Lord Preston, and for good reason. But now that she knew him, she saw the flaws in the stories. Yes, he was generous—but he weighed his gifts carefully, always concerned that they might end up being a mistakes. Yes, he believed in dignity for all—but he did not always know what made a person feel equal. He was no god, only a man.

A man she loved.

She remembered this kind of love from her early years of marriage. It was a love that made one stupid. She didn't want to eat unless it was beside him. She didn't want to think of anything except him. Even though everyone around her was grieving, Martha was full of joy because she *loved* Lord Preston.

When Caroline arrived two days after Mr. Maulvi's death to discuss the assembly, Martha did her best to snuff any hint of her feelings. She tried to excuse herself from the discussion entirely, but Caroline entreated her: "Please, Mrs. Bellamy, you know as much about a Thatcham assembly as I do. I would value your guidance."

They gathered in the garden drawing room. Martha was grateful; the last time she and Lord Preston had shared that space was on her first afternoon there, when they had been awkward and polite with each other. She pretended she was still that woman—a stranger to the Prestons, worried most of all about never finding a home among her family—as Lord Preston took a straight-backed chair at one end of the seating arrangement, his gaze not quite meeting Martha's. Among company he always grew stiff like this, and with Caroline especially they needed to be careful.

Over rose hip tisane, Caroline laid out her ideas for the assembly. There would be a spread of food provided by different households, music played by the musicians of Northfield Hall, and dancing called by Mr. Griswick.

"It all sounds very nice, but I would be happy to host it here. Are you quite sure the school building will do?" Lord Preston said as Caroline drew to a close.

"The people of Thatcham don't like coming all the way out here for an assembly. Not enough of them have carriages to make it convenient."

"And we have enough carriages for everyone from Northfield Hall to drive into Thatcham?"

Caroline set her lips in determination. "You may have your own celebration at Northfield Hall if you like, Papa, but Aunt Croft wants this party to be in Thatcham, where Uncle Maulvi *lived*, instead of here, where he *worked*."

Martha watched these words injure Lord Preston. His eyes dropped and his jaw worked, as if words were leaping to his tongue and he had to fight to keep them from getting out. She intervened: "It is beautiful that Mr. Maulvi belonged to two such rich communities. He was beloved by so many."

"Yes." Lord Preston looked at her with gratitude. "Well said, Mrs. Bellamy."

"Would you like to open the first set of dancing with Aunt Croft?" Caroline asked.

"She means to dance?" Lord Preston said sharply.

"She is the hostess. She wants to dance the opening set. It would be well done of you to dance with her."

They were approaching their customary bickering. Lord Preston said with an obvious attempt to calm the fire: "Of course I will dance with her. I am merely surprised she means to dance a month into mourning."

"People do all sorts of things while mourning," Caroline replied, and her eyes landed on Martha.

As if accused of some sin, Martha felt her cheeks heat, the absolute worst thing for them to do. She straightened in her seat like the rector's wife she had been for forty years and absolutely did *not* look at Lord Preston. "Mrs. Croft is a woman who follows her own compass. It is one of the things I admire about her."

"Indeed. And will you dance, Mrs. Bellamy?" asked Caroline.

Martha wondered what answer would bring an end to the interrogation. "I am a little old for dancing, I think."

"Nonsense. You are no older than Papa or Aunt Croft, and as we established, *they* will be dancing."

The girl was insatiable. Martha placated her: "Then, although I have never been very good at it, if someone asks, of course I shall accept."

Caroline smiled for only the briefest of moments. "However, Papa, I do not think *you* should ask Mrs. Bellamy. I'm afraid there is speculation in Thatcham about the nature of your relationship, and I should hate for more gossip to spread at Mr. Maulvi's memorial of all places."

Martha did not dare look at Lord Preston as a bolt of fear spiked down her spine.

It was one thing for Caroline to make her insinuations. It was another for her to name the gossip aloud.

Lord Preston sputtered: "I do not know what you are implying, Caroline, but I find your words offensive to both my character and Mrs. Bellamy's."

"I'm sorry, Mrs. Bellamy. I have the greatest respect for you. I speak only to protect you, not to shock you."

Martha forced herself to look at the girl. She was so young, dewy and brimming with the life growing inside her. Of course she meant no harm to Martha.

It was her father she wanted to injure.

Caroline wanted to see a shocked, offended widow. But Martha was a rector's wife, who had seen and survived her own share of scandals. She made an honest reply: "I am no stranger to the world.

I suspect such rumors were inevitable the moment I accepted the invitation to stay here. Still, I thank you for your care."

Caroline at last ducked her chin, the bluster that had allowed her to say such daring things disappearing. Martha was about to change the subject when Lord Preston said, "I'm sure such talk will disappear when Mrs. Bellamy moves to her niece's."

He did not look at her. Did that mean that he said it as a lie, knowing as Martha did that she still hadn't heard from Georgina?

Or did he want her to move on to clear his name from scandal?

"Yes," Martha agreed, because she would play along for him and him alone. "Perhaps I will even be gone before the date of the assembly."

"I'm sure there's no need for such a rush," Caroline said, pouring Martha more rose hip tisane. "Even if arrangements are made, you must stay for the assembly. Uncle Maulvi would want you there."

A kind sentiment, if untrue. Martha had barely even known the man. Even in these times of grief, people's lies were not always kind.

Chapter Fourteen

THERE WAS A TWIST in Martin's stomach that would not go away no matter how much ginger tisane he drank nor how many meals he reduced to clear broth and toasted bread. In Martha's company, it made his head perspire as he tried to balance the necessity of *not* taking her hands with his desperate desire to do just that. Out of her presence, it gave him the chills, almost as if he had a fever, as he braced for another accusation of impropriety.

He had batted away Caroline's as if he had the moral superiority of never so much as noticing that Martha Bellamy was a woman. He had survived that lie—but barely. The next time someone raised their eyebrow at the widow in his household, Martin was afraid he would confess to the truth of it all.

And then how would Caroline look at him?

How would everyone at Northfield Hall who had heard his warnings against licentious behavior listen to him?

How would Thatcham turn on him, the London papers pillory him, the respect he had worked so hard to earn disappear?

Martin would have to lie. But first, he could shore up his behavior. Starting that very evening after Caroline's visit, he distanced himself from Martha. Claiming stomachache—the beginnings of his terrible twist indeed already working upon him—he ordered supper in his private sitting room and declined her offer to join him. He did not go to her after the household went to bed. The next morning, he claimed he had business with Mr. Chow at the carpentry and insisted she remain behind to avoid the endless drizzle.

He kept finding excuses like that until, two days later, Martha carried a tea tray into the study and locked the door behind her. "Have I done something to offend you, sir, or is it the tales Caroline carried that have set you against me?"

His stomach twisted in the opposite direction, now a knot instead of a simple tangle. "I am not against you."

"You would not like to be alone with me, either."

"I am sensible of your reputation." Martin rose from where he sat and pulled shut the curtains on his bay window in case a groom or gardener was passing by.

"Fine. I should like to know what suddenly made you so 'sensible' and whether I have any say in the matter."

"You heard Caroline. There is already talk. I want to be your friend, Mrs. Bellamy, not the man who ruins your life."

Her fingers fisted so tightly that her knuckles turned white. "So it is back to Mrs. Bellamy, then."

It was the right thing to do. Yet Martin couldn't bear to see her retreat behind the stalwart mask she wore so carefully against the world. He rounded the desk and unwound her fingers so they entwined with his. "My heart beats the same for you no matter what name I call you."

Her lips softened ever so slightly. "That sounds like poetry when I am asking you to speak plainly to me."

Another accusation that landed all too true. Martin loosened his hold on her hands—but she gripped him tightly back. "It was fine when we were living quietly. With Maulvi's death and the upcoming assembly, there are eyes upon us now. When my daughters arrive, they will notice immediately any changes to my routine. Do you really want to invite everyone into our affair?"

"Then this is not the end? This is only until the assembly is over and no one is thinking of us again?" Martha softened a little, so that if he wanted to, he could have swept her into his arms. In fact, he *did* want to, but he resisted.

"I could not bear for this to be the end," he answered honestly.

She smiled, and he smiled, and they did kiss, since the door was already locked and the curtains drawn.

Martin sent Sophia a banknote in London, where she had been staying while John attended a family in Yorkshire, and she arrived within a matter of days. A week after that came Ellen, also on her own, as to travel with Max and their five children would have required too much preparation for them to attend the assembly. Northfield Hall went from being a quiet house for Martin and Martha to sneak around to a bustling household, with visitors calling on the family and Caroline coming to stay for several nights to maximize time with her sisters. Suppers now lasted over an hour, and the dining room resounded with lively conversation as Sophia tortured Ellen by playing devil's advocate. It was not the same as it ever had been, yet Martin almost had the sense that the clock had turned back and he had been restored to a younger self, to when he had known more firmly what kind of man he was.

"Your daughters are as different as different can be," Martha commented one morning when, by chance, it was just the two of them at breakfast. "I knew they did not have the same looks, but I did not realize their personalities were so different."

Martin had heard the comment dozens of times over the years from visitors and family friends. He knew what they meant: Ellen was sensible where Sophia was reckless, Caroline was headstrong where Ellen was principled, Sophia and Caroline both upset the apple cart of order to which Ellen clung. At the dining table, Ellen was well mannered, Sophia was witty, and Caroline expressive. And that was after one considered that Ellen was a slender, red-headed countess; Sophia a plump, brunette wanderer who happened to have an accoucheur husband; and Caroline the sturdy, blond wife of a glazier.

Yet to his eyes as their father, they were strikingly similar. They had strong opinions, and they weren't afraid to tell him when they disagreed. They had specific visions for their lives, and not even Ellen's was quite what Martin had expected for her. They carried their mother's heart—courageous, impatient, singular—while suffering his weakness of holding themselves to too high a standard.

They were Prestons, through and through.

"They are each determined to live as they see fit," he said to Martha. "To both my chagrin and my deep pleasure."

Her eyes crinkled with the hint of a smile. "It is clear they are very fond of each other, too, and you as well. Not all families can claim that."

With a pang, Martin remembered the terrible afternoon at Hope Hall, some three years ago, when his children had turned on him, accusing him of being unreasonable in trying to keep Caroline and Eddie apart.

He had raised children who loved each other unconditionally.

He wasn't sure that they extended that love to him any longer.

"It is a treat to have them home again," he replied. "A gift from Maulvi, though I wish he were here to enjoy their company, too."

"It is a treat for me, too, even though I didn't know them previously. They are lovely women." She reached out and, for the briefest of moments, squeezed his fingers. "It makes me glad to see you with your children."

He longed to keep her hand in his. There was nothing but joy in her words, her voice, her expression, yet the very sentiment came with sorrow, since she could never be reunited with Lucas. "They like you, I can tell."

She smiled with her full mouth, a little pink rising in her cheeks, and Martin had to push away his body's instinct to pull her into his lap and kiss those beautiful lips.

It was into this moment that Ellen entered. Martin jerked into perfect posture, though he had been doing nothing except mooning at Martha, and fixed his eyes on his plate. Martha busied herself refilling his cup with mint tisane. Ellen—who had been swanning into the room as if she owned the place—hesitated at the threshold. After a moment, she proceeded to the table, and thankfully, she did not comment on anything she might have observed, instead asking Martha a question about the fund for clergymen's widows.

Still, Martin was reminded that he could not risk even longing glances at Martha. He excused himself from the table and managed not to find himself in Martha's company until supper that day.

MARTHA WAS GROWING USED to living with two hearts beating inside her chest. One, for polite society, did not react too greatly to anyone's behavior, allowed her to enjoy the Preston daughters without being invested in them, and agreed that of course she should arrive at the assembly early with Caroline so as to avoid gossip sparked by entering with Lord Preston's group.

Her true heart beat on below. The one that at every second of the day waited for Lord Preston to glance her way or even mention her name; the one that kept her up each night, waiting for his knock though she knew it would never come. She understood all the reasons why they had to pretend they were nothing more than acquaintances. She *agreed* with the ruse and would have counseled any friend that it was the wisest course of action. Yet this heart of hers pumped blood through her veins each time there was the slightest chance she might for a second be alone with Lord Preston, because it craved him—the real him, not the adulterated version he presented for his daughters—once more.

She got little assurances that his heart, too, beat for her. Alone with him at breakfast, she saw his eyes soften the way they used to, before Ellen broke in upon them. Passing him in the corridor as she followed Sophia upstairs in search of a lost book, he swayed towards her just enough for their arms to brush. She was no longer seeing to his correspondence on a daily basis, but one afternoon he called her in to take a dictation for a long and boring letter to his solicitor that he could easily have written himself. Though he stood behind his desk the whole time, never close enough to touch her, the sweet way he thanked her—and the very fact that he had asked her to spend that hour with him—told Martha that he missed her as much as she missed him.

Once this assembly was over, and once his daughters had left Northfield Hall, they could return to their previous quiet arrangement. So long as gossip in Thatcham didn't take hold to frighten Lord Preston from ever speaking to her again.

With a sense of foreboding, then, Martha arrived at the schoolroom with Caroline to assist in setup. It being an informal assembly, the food was provided dish by dish from each family attending, and Martha was stationed at the buffet table to direct where the plates were laid. It surprised her how good it was to see these faces she had grown used to seeing every Sunday. Though Northfield Hall was only five miles from Thatcham, she had gone from weekly conversations in the churchyard to not catching up with these acquaintances at all.

Riding with Caroline in the carriage, Martha had felt brittle with anxiety, fearing that if any person so much as looked at her with too much meaning, she would crumble with embarrassment.

Instead, as the old barn filled with young mothers she had counseled on swaddling their babes and farmers who always paid a penny into the collection plate and the rabble-rousers who only came when Kenneth performed Communion, Martha relaxed into a version of herself she had thought had died with Lucas. These were more than the sheep her husband had shepherded; they were her friends, and she had missed them, and she was glad to see them after three months at Northfield Hall.

An ordinary assembly began its dancing when the musicians took up their instruments and the caller announced the first set. This one began with Mrs. Croft climbing atop a crate so she could better address the crowd.

"Thank you all for coming this evening. I know it seems strange to celebrate my Mr. Maulvi when we already miss him so much. This is what he asked of us. He lived here his whole life, first at Northfield Hall and these last forty years in Thatcham, and he admired most of all the way we neighbors care for each other. He would want us to spend tonight reminding each other that we will support each other through good and bad, that we will give each other grace in disagreements, and that we will not be mean about how we define 'we.' So, please, help us give his soul one last blessing by opening your purses for the Lascars, and join us in his favorite dance!"

Martha knew she wouldn't be dancing. Lord Preston wouldn't dare invite her, and no one else would think a sixty-two-year-old widow would want to. She helped herself to a cup of punch—spiked with some of Thatcham's local grain alcohol—to watch the country dance. Solemnly, Lord Preston led Mrs. Croft to the top of the line.

He didn't quite approve of any of this, even though it had been Mr. Maulvi's request. Martha felt a mix of amusement—that she could read him so easily—and protectiveness over him. Others might consider him judgmental; certainly, his daughters had little patience for his discomfort surrounding the assembly. To Martha's eyes, however, he was not trying to shame anyone. He was thinking too hard about everything, measuring each movement and word, and as a result, he seemed as remote and reserved as a lord should be.

She wished she could take his hand or lean her head against his shoulder. Anything to remind him he need not be perfect to be admired.

He was an elegant dancer, as one would expect. No doubt he had taken dancing lessons from a French master back in the days of young King George III. Through his sheer aptitude, he made Mrs. Croft look clumsy as she needed to be nudged to turn this way or prompted to cross the line in a diagonal. But the widow laughed at her own mistakes, earning a smile from Lord Preston, and the dancers all carried on merrily.

When the dance came to an end, Martha held her breath, hoping Lord Preston would next come to the table for some food. He could say a word to her without anyone finding it strange. They could smile at each other.

He turned to Ellen instead, and they headed to the top of the line for the next set. Martha released her exhale. At the next dance break, then.

Mr. Cropper, the publican, approached. "Would you be my partner, Mrs. Bellamy?"

"Oh." The offer surprised her so much that she could barely say anything, though she put her hand in his and allowed him to lead her into the formation. It was to be a quadrille, which Martha knew well from her younger days, and she said on a laugh to Mr. Cropper, "Good thing it's one I know, otherwise you'd be sorry you asked me."

"We danced it together at the Yuletide ball a few years ago, otherwise I wouldn't have dared," he replied. "I figured if Mrs. Croft is dancing, there is no reason why you shouldn't be, too."

The quadrille was slow enough to provide them time and breath to carry on conversation. "It was a nice idea of Mr. Maulvi's to ask us to celebrate instead of be morose," Martha said. "Or perhaps I only say that because I have spent so much of my last year closeted in mourning."

"It is just like him to make us do something strange for our own benefit," replied Mr. Cropper with a smile. "I remember my father complaining about all the favors Mr. Maulvi used to ask on behalf of Northfield Hall, only for them to turn out best for everyone involved. He had us add a private room with a window facing east, which seemed a huge expense, but we now have Mohammedans come out of their way from the turnpike so they may say their prayers in peace."

"I wish I'd known him better. He didn't call upon Mr. Bellamy or myself too often, since after all, he wasn't a churchman."

"He was a man who lived on his own terms, but without hurting a soul. In fact, more often than not, he would stop you on the street to tell you this or that reason he admired you. Everyone in this room has a story like that, I wager. He looked for the good in people, and he said it aloud when he found it."

Martha wondered what Mr. Maulvi would have said of her, had they known each other well enough for him to stop her on the street.

She wondered if Martin had confided in his friend about their affair, and whether Mr. Maulvi had approved.

The dance called for them to cross the line and change partners for a figure. Now Martha was with the wheelwright, a young man who was already sweating from the heat of dancing. To ease his obvious nerves, Martha asked, "Did you know Mr. Maulvi well?"

"Not well, ma'am, no, but he was the one who told me to stop dawdling and propose to my wife. I wasn't done with my apprenticeship, see, so we couldn't yet marry, but he said, 'Tell her you love

her and that you plan to marry her, and then it will all work out.'
And so I did, and she said she loved me too, and she waited for me.
If not for Mr. Maulvi, she might have married Joseph Duncan in
Reading, and then we'd both be miserable."

It was a beautiful story, and it filled the time they had together.
She and Mr. Cropper moved up the line while the wheelwright and
his partner moved down it. Mr. Cropper said, "I've often thought
of Mr. Maulvi as the heart of Northfield Hall. His lordship must
set the example about right and wrong, you see. Mr. Maulvi was the
one who saw gray, and never with judgment. He made allowances
for us to be human."

Martha chewed on this as they changed partners again for the
next figure. Before she had known him, she had considered Lord
Preston upright and reserved—the epitome of what a lord *should*
be, rather than rakish and loud and overly familiar with everyone.
He certainly held himself to high standards when he made decisions, but wasn't that right when his decisions impacted so many
people?

Did Lord Preston not allow the people around him to be human?

Did he not allow *himself* to be human?

She was so absorbed in this line of thought—and, perhaps,
growing winded from the quadrille—that she didn't notice that
Lord Preston and Ellen were the couple beside them until
Lord Preston met her in the middle of the line to dance the
change-in-partner figure. One moment she was woolgathering, and
the next, her eyes were filled with him.

"Good evening, Mrs. Bellamy." His words were stiff, but Martha felt his true feelings in the way he gripped her hand as if he would never let go.

"Mr. Cropper asked me to dance," she said. As the words came out, she cursed them as a waste of these precious instants they had together as figure partners.

"I'm glad. It can be good for the soul to dance."

"Everyone has wonderful things to say about Mr. Maulvi. I begin to think he was an angel who walked among us."

Martin smiled. Her breath stopped for that moment. She was so accustomed to him in his home, but here he was in a formal black evening coat, his cravat perfectly starched and tied to frame his chin. He was so handsome that she wanted to kiss him right there on the dance floor.

"He inspired Adam Grigg to confess his love to his sweetheart so that she would wait to marry him. Isn't that romantic?"

"Indeed, Maulvi was quite the romantic."

Which wasn't quite the same thing as agreeing with her. Martha added, "I think he was right that it is better to be courageous and honest than to stay silent and hope your love story will work itself out."

Lord Preston tugged her closer, which was part of the dance, and didn't say anything.

He held himself to too-high standards. He didn't allow himself to be human. He did not consider that he *could* be in love because he did not think he *should* be in love.

And, Martha realized, he had lost his best friend, who would have told him to listen to his heart instead of gossip.

She wouldn't do it now, in the middle of the dance floor with everyone from Thatcham and Northfield Hall watching. But as they stared at each other through the tune of the quadrille, Martha resolved that when this was all over, she would not permit him to retreat to the quiet arrangement they had enjoyed before. When they finally were able to speak plainly again, she would tell him she loved him madly—and see what waited on the other side of that confession.

CHAPTER FIFTEEN

Martin had never been one for parties, and he was especially glad when Maulvi's assembly ended. It was too strange to dance in a room full of mourners and too hard to try to avoid looking Martha's way. He wanted to be done with all of it: the obligation of displaying his feelings for Maulvi, the small details about Thatcham villagers he needed to remember of which normally Maulvi would have reminded him, the press of so many people in the barn, the threat of scrutiny if he so much as smiled at Martha.

They had danced together for only a moment, during an early quadrille, yet when Ellen had reclaimed him as her partner, she had given him so searching a look Martin thought he must have kissed Martha in front of the whole assembly.

That was, of course, what he had *wanted* to do. If he could have had his way, he would have pulled two overstuffed chairs into a corner of the room and sat with Martha all night. That being impossible, he would have settled for dancing with her as his sole partner through all the sets of quadrilles and minuets and reels. That being ridiculous, he would have eaten his supper beside her to hear her observations on the evening.

As it was, he could not even ride home in the same carriage as her. To avoid talk, Martha climbed into the gig with Mr. and Mrs. Chow to return to Northfield Hall, while Martin took the family carriage with his daughters and Eddie. When they got home, he would have to surrender her to her bedroom without following her in, for on this night of all nights, Sophia and Ellen and Caroline would likely stay up talking and catch anyone sneaking through the corridors.

He was a horrid old man to consider threatening Martha's reputation like that, anyhow. He knew the correct way to behave, and it was high time he showed her the respect she was due, which was to *not* take advantage of her just because she told him he could.

He had bid everyone goodnight and retreated to his dressing room when his daughters knocked on his door.

At first, he thought it was only Ellen, and he assumed he had dropped something in the corridor as he shrugged out of his coat. Then Sophia and Caroline followed her into the room, and true fear gripped his stomach.

"Is there bad news from abroad?" he asked—devil that he was, hoping this was about a topic that had nothing to do with him.

"No, nothing like that," Ellen assured him. She stood by his washstand, one hand on its smooth wooden mirror post. Sophia guarded the door while Caroline seated herself on his sofa.

Martin couldn't remember the last time his children had been in his dressing room. When Lolly was alive, probably. He had the strange urge to usher them out, as if they were intruding on him naked and not properly ashamed.

"We are concerned about you, Papa," said Ellen, her voice gentle yet firm, no doubt the tone she used to warn her children from foolish ventures. "Caroline told us about the rumors of an intrigue between you and Mrs. Bellamy. I thought for sure it was vicious gossip, but what I saw with my own two eyes alarms me."

Martin withdrew a dressing robe from his armoire. It was not his favorite—that one lay in wait for him across the foot of his bed—but it gave him some armor as he defended himself. "What on earth could you have seen that alarmed you?"

"Mrs. Bellamy is in love with you."

The words resounded in his ears, or perhaps that was his heart pounding doubly hard. "Then surely this is a conversation you should be having with her."

Ellen grew shrill. "Mrs. Bellamy is in love with you, and you haven't a care for her reputation!"

"Perhaps Papa is in love with her," Sophia suggested.

Martin's head spun. Of all his children, Sophia was the one he would expect to understand that his arrangement with Martha need have nothing to do with love. He couldn't see any reply except: "Of course I am not in love with her."

"Everyone knows you two are carrying on," said Caroline. "Mrs. Chow told me she thinks it is wonderful, and she wouldn't say anything about it if she didn't know it was absolutely true."

"Even the mighty Mrs. Chow can be wrong sometimes." He heard how bitter his words sounded, and he regretted them—of course he did, for not only was he lying, but he was denigrating poor Mrs. Chow as he did so! She had nothing to do with him and Martha; she had very little to do with him and Caroline, for that matter; he wished he were a better man. Since he wasn't, he added, "It is beyond my imagination that you three would consider this a worthy topic of discussion, much less at this time of night. Let us go to bed and forget about it."

Ellen jerked away—giving Martin hope that she might heed him—but Sophia remained by the door. "We haven't anything against you taking a lover, Papa. It's the manner in which you do it that matters. Mrs. Bellamy has nothing but her reputation to live on. You mustn't look at her in the middle of an assembly as if you want to tear her clothes off."

Caroline objected to this with a sound of disgust, and Martin couldn't help but growl at those words coming from his daughter.

"More importantly," Ellen said, "you mustn't make promises you won't keep to that poor woman. I am quite sure she thinks you will marry her, Papa."

"Oh yes, if you were to marry her, it wouldn't matter how you look at her," Sophia amended, "but as it seems you are behaving like every other man and denying your own sin, you really must have a care."

"Do you want to marry her?" Caroline asked.

Martin didn't know how the conversation had gotten so out of hand. "Of course I do not want to marry her. You are letting gossip chase the sense out of your heads. I am a responsible man. I would not take advantage of a poor, lonely widow when she is my guest. What, do you think I have been sneaking into her bedroom at night to ravish her? How can you accuse me of such things?"

He felt physically ill. His hands trembled, his skin grew clammy, and if he had to say another word, he thought he might vomit.

Caroline threw her hands up in the air. "I don't believe you, Papa! *We* don't believe you. Maybe when we were younger, we would have swallowed your lie, but we are not children. I really wanted you to admit to it because then, at least, I could go to sleep knowing my father is an honest man. Instead, I just have confirmation of what I already knew. You're a coward and a liar and you won't stand up for half the lofty principles you always claim." Pushing herself to her feet, she snarled at her sisters, "I told you that it wasn't worth trying," and barreled out of the room.

Martin counseled himself not to say anything, for he had learned in the past few years that this was the emotional state in which he only said harmful things.

Besides, there was no defense against Caroline's accusations.

"We are not trying to shame you, Papa," Sophia said, her voice calm. "We are trying to help you see the situation as others do so that you may make the right decisions. Everyone knows Mrs. Bellamy has lived here alone with you for the past few months."

"Alone with a dozen servants!" Martin objected.

"You asked her to be your private secretary and have been locking yourself away in the study with her."

"Only if you mean 'locking' euphemistically," he lied. "Anyone can enter at any time."

"Leyla told me she *did* try to enter once to take away your lunch tray and that all the doors were locked," said Ellen quietly.

"Besides," said Sophia, "you have never needed a secretary before. Like George III, we always said, didn't we?"

Her words were not a question. Martin summoned a logical defense. "She has been helping me consider a very private matter that I did not want anyone to interrupt."

Sophia rolled her eyes. "Please, Papa, do not take us for idiots."

"I am not lying. She has been helping me with my will. Perhaps you can understand why I did not want Leyla or the Chows or anyone else to overhear."

"What could you have to discuss about your will that is so private? The land is entailed and the money..." Sophia suddenly frowned. "You are leaving us money, are you not?"

He was so relieved to be telling the truth that he continued to do so: "That is what I have been weighing."

"You have been weighing whether or not we merit the family legacy?" In an instant, Sophia went from calm to angry, the old anger that Martin used to imagine shook the entire house. "Of course, why should we expect any money from you? We are only your daughters. We cannot inherit Northfield Hall. We cannot fight beside you in Parliament. I thought at least I could expect that being a Preston meant I wouldn't have to worry about money to live a modestly comfortable life. But I should have known better. After all, you hardly even agree to send me the coach money to visit you."

"This is not a question of your merit, Sophia. I must consider the legacy of Northfield Hall."

"Oh, Northfield Hall will sustain itself whether you send me an extra few pounds for travel or not."

Martin felt justified to rejoin, "You are the one who chose to marry a man without a fortune. You mustn't be shocked that you must now make do with a different lifestyle than that to which you were accustomed."

"And yet if Caroline were to ask you for that money, you would give it to her without a question. If Ellen needed it, you would send it immediately. It is only I you are stingy with because I am the one you have always found wanting!" To his surprise, Sophia's eyes reddened with tears. "I should have learned my lesson when you left me to rot at Robin Abbey rather than come to my defense."

The anecdote was from so long ago that Martin almost didn't remember what she referred to. "Did I not send Max in my stead?"

"It should have been my father." Sophia glared at him, the tears gone, replaced by her fury. "I don't care that I am the thorn in your side who refuses to live by your rules. That doesn't change the fact that I'm your daughter, Papa, and I *am* worthy, and I will not let you treat me as a burden any longer."

"Sophia!"

She whirled away, and he could not follow because Ellen remained, stiff as a rod. Martin said helplessly, "How am I to convince her none of that is true?"

"Perhaps by admitting what *is* true."

Stuck on the accusation that he had not helped Sophia in her hour of need, he said, "I thought I had a chance at passing a bill to abolish slavery once and for all. If I had left, it would have lost all its momentum."

"It didn't pass anyway."

"I didn't have the benefit of knowing that."

"You were not the bill's only sponsor, but you were—and are—Sophia's only father."

He swallowed Ellen's words, trying very hard not to drown them out with his own defenses. "She was always getting herself into scandals. I didn't realize that was the one she would remember."

Ellen gazed at him with hardly any emotion. "And what of Mrs. Bellamy, Papa? What is true now?"

Martin had no choice but to stick to his earlier denial. "None of it. I swear to you, Ellen, none of it."

Oh, he hated himself for saying it. A part of him wished he could go back and admit to the affair as soon as Caroline had mentioned it in the garden drawing room weeks ago. Then, at least, his daughters could not accuse him of lying, though they would know all his other terrible deeds.

A sheen of tears fell over Ellen's eyes. "I learned a long time ago that you were fallible, Papa, yet still I thought you were constant. But now—" She searched him with those heartbreaking eyes. "I don't even recognize you."

Martin reached out for her, but she, too, deserted him.

He did not have the courage to follow any of them.

He did not have the words to put anything right.

He did not even have the strength to make an honest man of himself.

And it was this terrible version of a man that Martha encountered when she entered the dressing room.

Chapter Sixteen

Martha had only gotten as far as removing her boots when she heard the raised voices in Lord Preston's suite. Northfield Hall was not a house through which sound carried easily, yet Martha could distinctly make out Caroline's voice, rising to a screech. And she could not ignore the thunder of feet rushing down the corridor, one pair at a time. She cracked open her door in time to see Ellen walking away, a hand pressed to her face.

Whatever had just occurred was not a happy family discussion.

She did not waste time lacing up her boots again before slipping into the corridor. Knocking softly on the door to Lord Preston's apartment, she let herself in. He had never invited her into these rooms. The first chamber, a sitting room with a threadbare silk-upholstered settee and a bookcase, was empty. Martha crossed through its door and found herself in the bedroom. A massive, dark wood bed took up most of the room, its heavy posts rising towards the ceiling and cloaked in a dark velvet canopy. Looking at it pressed her lungs so close she wasn't sure she could breathe; in any case, she turned towards the candlelight beckoning from the dressing room, where she discovered Lord Preston standing still.

He wore a dressing gown over the fine wool waistcoat, linen shirt, and black pantaloons of his formal suit, his hair tied back in a queue by a ribbon. Her heart might have skipped a double beat because of how handsome he was. Or perhaps it was the expression on his face: bereft, betrayed, bewildered.

She rushed to take his hands, if only to give him something to lean on. "Your daughters have upset you."

Lord Preston looked at her, but his gaze was so distant that Martha wasn't sure he saw her. "They accuse me of misusing you."

"Why? We hardly even spoke tonight."

"They think you are in love with me and that I am taking advantage of you."

Now Martha's heart hammered so loud she could barely think straight. She hadn't planned to make her confession tonight. She thought she would have another week at least to practice what she would say—to find the courage.

But what was the point in being precious about it? Lord Preston needed to hear it from her now. "I *am* in love with you."

Saying the words aloud buoyed her with warmth like a summer breeze. She almost laughed to hear them from her own lips.

Had she ever said so wonderful a thing in all her life?

"I am in love with you," she said again, grinning.

"Then I am taking advantage of you." If Martha's confession was summertime, then Lord Preston's words came from the depths of winter.

It was not the response she had expected. "No, you are not."

"This was never supposed to be a love affair."

That did not mean he could not have fallen in love with her, in return. He needed time to consider it. He needed a chance to realize it did not mean he had done anything wrong. "You never misled me," she assured him, trying desperately to keep control of her breath. "Aren't I the one who said we need only be friends?"

He stepped backward. Martha was painfully aware that he was no longer looking at her.

"I meant to reassure you, but I can see it has been a long night," she said. "We should discuss this another time."

"It can't go any farther. It was never supposed to go this far."

Martha insisted, "Let's discuss this tomorrow, or next week after your daughters have left."

He opened a drawer in his armoire and withdrew a leather purse. Martha wanted to pull his hands away to stop him from whatever he was doing. He unfolded a banknote, looked at it in the candlelight for a long moment, and then handed it to her. "It would be best if you remove yourself to the Fox and Hound tomorrow. This should cover your expenses for the foreseeable future, and if ever you need more, I'll arrange it."

It was a note for one hundred pounds—more than Kenneth's yearly tithes in Thatcham. Martha did not want Lord Preston's money. She had never wanted it. She was neither whore nor courtesan nor mistress; she was only a woman who loved a man.

Yet shaking hands could not return it. "I never asked for anything from you."

"It is the least of what I owe you."

She shouldn't have come into his apartment. If only she had left him to his inner sanctum—even though his daughters had broken his spirit—then she would not now be taking his money like a London courtesan.

She could have kept her love to herself. He need never have known. And then they could have continued, and she could still have had him, and she would not need to disappear to an inn in Theale or Georgina's house in London.

"I don't want your money," she whispered.

"Mrs. Chow will assist you with the travel arrangements. You should take the carriage. Theale is far enough away that the gig would be an uncomfortable ride."

At last, he looked at her again. His posture was rigid and cold, with all the hauteur of a peer of the realm.

Martha couldn't tell if there was any emotion in his eyes, or if she only wanted there to be.

He said, "You mustn't blame yourself. I should never have allowed this to happen. All the fault lies with me."

"It was my idea to begin with." And Martha suddenly remembered Lucas saying the same thing to her when she warned him off getting his head turned by Lady Imogen: *Mother, you cannot blame her when I am the one courting her.*

She had cursed him for being foolish. She had beseeched the heavens to tell her how she had raised a son who made such terrible mistakes.

And now Martha knew. She and Lucas had the same doomed heart.

At least, if she had to lose Lord Preston, she was a little bit closer to her lost son.

Martha found it in her to say one last thing. "It doesn't do any good when you are so hard on yourself." Then, holding fast to the banknote, she removed herself from his rooms.

CHAPTER SEVENTEEN

S HE DEPARTED WITH ALL the dignity she could muster. For appearance's sake, she pretended to have at long last received the letter from Georgina inviting her to come make a home in London. After packing her meager inventory of belongings, she descended to take breakfast with the family—but the footman informed her they had all elected to take the meal in their rooms. She lingered at the table as Mrs. Chow called for the carriage, and then she waited in the doorway as Boyle packed her bag into the coach.

Lord Preston did not come down to make things right. He did not send a note of apology with Mrs. Chow. He did not even show himself to say farewell as the servants assembled to wish her a safe journey.

His absence made it easier to leave—frankly, made it easier to be angry instead of devastated as she climbed into his fancy carriage with his hundred-pound banknote sewn safely into the hem of her petticoat.

She had not asked anything of him. She had not accused him of anything. She had not done anything except bare her heart to him, and he repaid her by sending her away.

Perhaps everyone else was right and he was not the man he claimed to be.

As she settled onto the carriage bench—back stiff so as to demonstrate perfect posture to anyone looking—she got her final glimpse of Lord Preston. He stood in the bay window of his study, just behind the gauzy window curtains that screened for privacy while letting in sunlight. At the moment, the sky was steel gray and shedding a light, unpleasant drizzle of icy rain. He was hardly more than a shadow behind that layer of white linen, a statue of a man with his hands frozen behind his back, his head bowed as if in prayer.

For the briefest of moments, their gazes collided, and Martha forgot to be angry, so desperate was she for him to make everything right.

And then the horses began to walk and the carriage began to roll and Martha was pulled away from him.

She allowed herself to cry in the carriage. If he had died, she would have been allowed to sob in a bedroom without question, or at least keen with the village as they all mourned their lost lord. But he was not dead; he simply no longer wanted to have anything to do with her. And so this grief, unlike all her others, must remain secret. When her tears became more audible, more like sobs, she pulled herself together, gasping in air until she was calm again, so that Boyle wouldn't hear.

By the time they arrived at the Fox and Hound, Martha had tucked her handkerchief into her sleeve and returned to being the somber woman she had been before Northfield Hall. She secured a room for a week with her own ten shillings and bid Boyle farewell with a tip of a half crown.

"We'll miss you around the Hall," he said gruffly, tugging at his cap as if she were a great lady deserving of his respect.

"Everything has its season. Take good care of yourself."

She wondered if Lord Preston would ask Boyle how she looked as he took his leave. Should she call Boyle back and leave some final words with him for Lord Preston to interpret?

But she didn't know what she wanted to say, other than *Take it back, please.*

She made a routine for herself at the Fox and Hound as she endured the week. Breakfast—bread, cheese, and actual tea—in her room. A walk around the green, during which she allowed herself to stop in at one shop a day. In the afternoons, she sat in the inn's parlor with her embroidery hoop. She took supper in the common room and then retired to her bedchamber, where she read by candlelight before forcing herself to at least *try* to sleep.

It wasn't much of a life, but it afforded her a heartbeat within which to consider her options.

She yearned to return Lord Preston's hundred pounds. Even though she hadn't heard from Georgina, she could go to Battersea and join the family of seven in a bed that might well be in the same room as those five children. It was the proper place for an old widow, the only place where Martha could hope to have people take notice of her as she grew weaker and weaker.

Try as she might—and she tried especially hard that week—Martha couldn't imagine herself in Georgina's family. She couldn't see herself disappearing into a corner of chaos, nor could she summon excitement at the prospect of watching over all those children. There would be so much life in that house, if it was even a house; Martha wasn't sure she had the wherewithal to sustain it.

If she hadn't been at Northfield Hall, perhaps she could have been happy with Georgina. But she *had* gone to Northfield Hall; she *had* unlocked her heart to Lord Preston, for better or worse, and now the hopes and dreams and loves that had lain dormant inside her for years were awakened again. Martha did not merely want to survive. She wanted to thrive. She wanted to be as full and happy and flawed a person as she had been when Lucas was alive.

Which meant, she concluded as her days at the Fox and Hound drew to a close, that she needed to do what she had not done all these years.

She needed to say a proper goodbye to Lucas.

And to do that, she needed to accept Lord Preston's bitter gift.

A ND SO HIS LIFE reverted to what it should be. A quiet Northfield Hall, emptied of his children, who had seen fit to build lives very different and apart from his. Plodding winter days full of correspondence and decisions. Cold reviews of the estate to discover the latest problems sprouting on top of the ones just fixed.

It was the right thing to send Martha away. It had been wrong to dally with her—wrong to kiss those fingertips, unbraid that hair, taste that delicate skin—and so it was right to tear himself away from her, though the rip was violent and painful. When she left, he checked her bedchamber, fearing she had left him a final note that a maid might find, and took in his last breath of her scent. There was only a lace glove, lost beneath the bed, which she had often worn to supper with his daughters in that last month. Martin tucked it into his pocket, in case she wrote upon discovering its loss.

He didn't hear from her, but he did keep the glove close. He didn't allow himself to think of her, but he did stroke those lace fingers when he was alone in his study. He didn't permit his thoughts to wander to Theale, but he did, every so often, press the lace to his nose and inhale the sensible scent of Martha.

She deserved a much better final chapter to her life than as mistress to a hypocritical old man.

He did his best not to think about his children, either. Neither Ellen, who did not recognize him, nor Sophia, who did not accept his love, wrote to him after leaving Northfield Hall; he heard instead from their husbands that they had arrived safely home. Caroline, citing exhaustion in her final months of expecting, remained in Thatcham instead of coming for Sunday dinners. Nor were there letters from Benjamin in Ireland, and Nate wrote from Portsmouth to say his wife was too ill to travel to Berkshire for Christmas after all.

In other words, Martin had been rejected wholesale by all five of his children. He had tasted this before, when they had rallied behind Caroline in her quest to marry Eddie. The difference now was that he did not have the heart to fight his way back into their good graces. Perhaps he was the hypocrite they accused him of being. Martin could admit to himself that they might very well be right. They must be, to decide he was so unworthy of their love that they could not forgive him.

This time, he would waste no energy trying to convince them he was not a monster. For after all, he was! He was a lecher who took advantage of a poor widow. He was a tartar who ignored his daughters in crisis. He was a narcissist who only helped the needy in order to convince the world he was a good person. He did not actually know each person living at Northfield—not even their names, when Maulvi could have told him at least two sentences about every soul!—nor did he have the appetite to take meals in the dining hall to meet them all. And after all those years that he had abandoned his family for the parliamentary season in London to work on abolition bills, British plantations still owned slaves in the West Indies. Had Martin ever truly been willing to do what it would take to bring about abolition, or did he only give voice to the idea without forcing the change through his government?

If his children considered him a monster, Martin decided, then it was time to finalize his will once and for all. He summoned his solicitor from London to finish it before Christmas. The estate, entailed by law to Benjamin, would remain in the family. The money would be put into a trust, to be used only for improvements to Northfield Hall. His children, who wanted nothing from him, would be permitted to select any furniture or clothing about which they were sentimental.

It was, all in all, a simple will. His solicitor presented the final draft for him to sign in the late afternoon; Martin called in Mr. Chow as his witness; and the whole chore was completed by sunset. Martin wondered why he had wasted so much time deliberating, why he had forced Martha to listen to his whining about how difficult it was to decide.

Alone in his study, he unlocked the cabinet in which he hid his father's rum. He had stopped drinking it thirty years ago, when he and Lolly had turned Northfield Hall into an estate which lived off its own produce, but he was a known monster now, and so he might as well revel in his hypocrisy. The first sip burned his throat—he was accustomed to home-brewed wines and ales—but the second one cleansed him, and by the third, he felt almost cheerful at the idea of ridding himself of pretenses.

Why should he contort himself into a good person he clearly was not?

From Martha's desk—his secretary's desk, that was—he removed all the notes she had made for him about previous drafts. Selecting the one on which she had written *Legacy to family,* Martin sauntered over to the hearth and fed the paper to the fire. The flames, which had been smoldering on their coals, leapt at the kindling, curling the paper into hot orange licks within seconds.

Removing the metal fire screen for better access, he picked up the next piece of paper—part of an early draft containing instructions to his children on how to use the money he designated for them—and touched it to the flames. In an instant, it, too, was ashes.

Strange, how satisfying it was to watch his ideas destroyed. Martin took a burning sip of rum and threw in another note. Its flame was desultory and quick. Martin wanted something more dramatic. He took a sheaf of six papers and lit them in the fire. They lasted longer, twitching this way and that as the heat ripped them in two. Martin liked that; he added the whole remaining stack of drafts next and watched his words disappear.

Almost dancing with glee, Martin swigged rum as he pulled out more papers from the desk Martha had used: copies of correspondence he had sent that he would never need to reference, letters he had received from complete strangers whom he had no intention of helping, solicitations from merchants with whom he had no interest in doing business. With each paper added to the fire, he treated himself to a sip of rum. There went his misplaced promises; here disappeared any notion that he was a man whom others should admire. When he finished with these papers and when he finished with the rum, he would emerge the truest version of himself: a Martin who was concerned only with what brought *him* satisfaction.

He ran out of papers from the secretary's desk, and so he turned to his own. He could not throw away records of the estate, nor correspondence regarding Parliament, but here—here was a note he had written to Martha, before Maulvi had died! Not so much a note as a poem, and not so much a poem as drivel; even sober Martin had known better than to show it to her. He carried it to the fire. For good measure, he poured rum on the flames to make them leap.

What a fool he was. What a self-important idiot. What a useless piece of fluff. After all this time, had he abolished slavery? Had he reformed Parliament to truly represent the people of Britain? Even his successes this past session were too little too late, written in the blood of people already hung, already transported, or—like Martha's poor son—already buried at a crossroads.

He turned his back to the fire to find more kindling. He would have to find something other than paper soon, for there wasn't much else he could afford to lose. His hand landed on Martha's glove in his pocket—but no, *that* he wouldn't burn.

He seized the letter Max had sent to tell Martin that Ellen was safely home. Hurling it into the hearth, Martin threw more rum after it, yearning for the beautiful blue that came from flames so hot and intense that they broke free from the color of fire.

They broke free. From color—and from the hearth. They roared forward, catching the fringe of the carpet that protected the hardwood floor. Martin rushed to stamp them out; now the fire leapt to the low-hanging tail of his jacket. A heat he had never before known breathed against his skin. Panicking, he twisted out of the coat, letting it fall to the ground, to escape the blaze. But as it fell, it spread its flame to the upholstered chair, and the embers in the carpet grew courageous and began to spread.

Martin reached for the bucket of sand kept by the hearth to bank the fire. But the air was fast filling with smoke, and the sand did nothing as he threw it on the paper-and-rum-fueled coal. He had no choice to scream "Water!" and "Fire!" and then he had no choice but to race from the room.

"Fire!" he screamed again. He couldn't remember what time of day it was, whether the servants would be sleeping in the attics. He seized the grandfather clock in the foyer and shook it until its bells rang in an eerie clamor. Running to the back corridor, he shouted, "Fire!"

He didn't see anyone. If he was going to stop the fire, he needed to find someone. If he was going to escape the fire, he needed to leave.

Martin ran to the garden drawing room, instead. He seized the portrait of Lolly from above the mantel; with it under his arm, he picked up the pens Ellen had made for his fortieth birthday, the book of poems Benjamin had presented him, Sophia's watercolor of the pond, Nate's letters from the navy, and Caroline's printed essays. He raced into the back garden and deposited his treasures beyond the hedge. He shouted again, "Fire!"

This time, when he ran back into Northfield Hall, he found the footmen racing towards the study. "Who is upstairs?" he asked. "Is anyone upstairs?"

They didn't know. And so Martin ran up the stairs—ignoring the way his lungs wheezed and his heart seized—to the top story. "Fire!

Get out!" He pounded on the walls loud enough to wake the dead. He opened all the doors to make sure there was no one there—and found one maid for his trouble. "Get out now!"

He could think of a hundred things he wanted to save from his and his children's bedrooms. But there was no time. He tripped down the staircase on his way back to the ground floor, catching himself on the banister. Three footmen were working in a chain to fight the fire now. It had spread through the door of the study into the back corridor. Coughing, Martin tried to help the men, but he couldn't bear the weight of the water buckets.

"Get to safety, sir!" shouted Jacques.

He wanted to protest—wanted to stay—it was his calamity and therefore his to fix. But strong arms seized him from behind and pulled him into the cold December night.

Mr. Chow. "Let us see to the fire, and you stay here."

"I can't let you in there," Martin argued. Chow was at least the same age, and besides, had a family that loved him. "It's my fire, not yours."

Chow glared at him. They had met at nighttime, like this, when all Martin could see was the shadows of the other man's face. Then, Chow had been begging for help. Now, Martin was the desperate one—but so much more undeserving than Chow had ever been.

"Keep my wife safe," Chow said.

Martin was drunk and weak, and so he had no choice but to accept the order as his friend ran back into Northfield Hall. The entire back corridor was lit in terrible red flames; the chain of men passing water buckets from the well to the hall kept getting longer, yet the fire kept getting bigger. The air filled with smoke. Martin wrapped a handkerchief around his mouth and still, he couldn't help coughing.

"We should take shelter, sir," Mrs. Chow said. "We can take people into the cottages for the night."

She was right, though the night hardly felt cold in the face of such a blaze. "Yes," Martin agreed, "take everyone away. Let them get rest. We will need courage and strength in the morning."

"And you, sir," she said. "Come to my cottage. I will make up a bed for you."

"No, thank you, ma'am." Martin could not disobey her husband, who had good sense on his side in keeping a feeble old man away from the disaster. But he *would* not obey her, no matter that the air was smoky and the winter night dangerous. "I must bear witness."

"When it is over, then," she said. "When it is over, Caroline will want to know that you stayed with us."

"For Caroline," he agreed. Mrs. Chow led the group of house servants down the dark paths leading to cottages that—God willing—would remain safer than the Hall.

Martin remained where he was, just on the far edge of the gravel driveway, and watched his home burn down. The rooms where he had been born, grown up, and raised his own children. The remnants of the first baron's home, built in the Elizabethan era. The last vestiges of Lolly. The books and records and manifests of his lifetime of efforts. The paintings he had brought back from his travels; the watercolors his children had painted; the furniture inherited generation by generation.

The flames lasted through the night, their smoke obscuring the stars and the moon. It was not until dawn that the fire finally drowned under the relentless buckets of water. At last, the chain of men broke up, each of them falling exhausted onto the frosted grass. The early morning sunlight illuminated what was left: the skeleton of Northfield Hall, the scars of Northfield Hall, the memory of Northfield Hall.

And Martin saw, at last, his legacy.

Chapter Eighteen

D ECEMBER WAS A BAD time to travel in any part of England, but Martha made do and arrived in Bath with her baggage and her bones all in one piece. She took a room in a lodging house on Seymour Street recommended by a guidebook, where the other guests were also widows or spinsters with limited means. The landlady served breakfast and supper in a common room which was always too hot from an overfed fire, while the bedrooms were ice cold, but Martha was grateful that at least she had a room to herself.

During her three-day journey to Bath, she had set herself an itinerary. Her first stop was at the High Street Bank to establish an account with Lord Preston's banknote. If it made her a courtesan, then she was a courtesan; she was too old and life too hard for her to eschew his money on principle.

Then, with five pounds in her purse and the rest secured in the bank, Martha followed her firmest link to Lucas. She had received one letter from him while he and Lady Imogen lived in Bath, and though she had burned it upon receipt, the address was seared into her memory: 18 Corn Street.

She walked from the bank, though it took the better part of an hour and her feet began to ache. This was not the well-to-do part of Bath where the best of London retreated for health remedies; as Martha trudged along the cobblestone street, the buildings grew shabbier, older, and smaller. Number 18 Corn Street was a narrow two-story house, its roof chipped. Its front door stood an inch open because it was too swollen to shut in its frame. Martha tried to imagine Lucas arriving there, his skin robust with youth, his heart happy with Lady Imogen at his side. She couldn't: everything on Corn Street was dreary, and her son didn't belong there.

The door opened, and a crone of a man glared at her. "Are you looking for a room or are you looking for trouble?"

Her breath caught in her lungs. This man was older than her; if this was still a lodging house, then could he have been the proprietor a decade ago, too? Holding out a shilling, she said, "I'm hoping you have a memory of my son."

He took the coin. "A fair number of sons cross my way."

"This was in 1812. He lived here with his wife, a young lady. She had a baby, and both she and the baby died." Martha didn't want to have to say what had happened next.

A hint of sympathy snuck into the man's expression. "We've had many guests like that over the years."

"He was blond and tall. He had a scar on the back of his right hand from getting caught on a fishing hook as a boy."

The landlord shook his head.

She should leave. What memory could this man have, if she did manage to remind him of Lucas? But the part of her that wanted to resurrect her son said: "He shot himself."

At last, recognition lit the man's eyes. Immediately, he looked away. "Ah, we've had a few of those too, but I reckon I remember your son. Gave us a false name, which we only discovered when they looked through his papers to notify a next of kin."

He and Lady Imogen had borrowed Martha's maiden name, Aveling, for their charade. "Was he happy? Before his wife died, I mean?"

The man rubbed the coin in his palm. "Yes, he was, ma'am. Your son was happy."

Happy.

She could tell the man was saying what he thought she wanted to hear. He didn't remember Lucas except for her son's terrible end. Before that, Lucas had just been another dissolute young man hiding from reality on Corn Street.

But she wanted Lucas to have been happy. She wanted to imagine him and Lady Imogen lighting up the dilapidated house with their bliss at being husband and wife. She wanted to hear they had been planning a beautiful future together, and that they didn't mind being cut off from their families or forced to use a false name.

She wanted joy for his last months on this earth.

Thanking the man, she walked back to her room on Seymour Street. There was plenty of time left in the day, but she needed a rest before she faced the next task on her itinerary.

The following morning, bolstered by a cup of boiling-hot tea and a bowl of lukewarm porridge, Martha found the coroner's office in the Guild Hall. Here, a lone clerk who looked about the age of eighteen manned the desk. He greeted her with polite curiosity. "May I help you, ma'am?"

Martha had rehearsed her words as she walked over. Faced with a fellow human, however, her speech died in her mouth.

Was she really supposed to reveal to this child that her son had destroyed himself?

"I am looking for records of my son's death in 1812," she said instead. "Does this office have such records?"

The boy frowned. "What kind of records do you mean exactly?"

"I would like to know where he is buried."

Now the boy leaned backward, judgment descending over his young face. "If we didn't know his name, then he would be in the potter's field."

The shame that Martha knew so well, had lived with so deeply this past decade, surged up like floodwaters and almost overwhelmed her. A few months ago, it *would* have overwhelmed her.

But Lord Preston had told her there was no reason to compound the crime with shame.

"The coroner knew his name. He was buried at a crossroads. I want to know which crossroads."

The clerk gulped. "We don't keep records of that."

Of course they didn't. They could not allow families to memorialize the suicides; they could not permit a mother to grieve her child. Martha lifted her chin in the face of his scorn. "But surely someone knows which crossroads they used. Or is there a body under every crossroads in this city?"

"I don't know, ma'am."

"And you cannot think of anyone I should ask?"

He shook his head. "I'm sorry, ma'am."

Another man lying to her, telling her what he deemed appropriate for her to hear. Or was he simply trying to defeat her? Was he so invested in the belief that Lucas deserved no mourners that he would engineer this outcome by declaring ignorance?

Martha couldn't force him to tell her anything. But she was far older than this boy, and she knew he was not her last resort.

And, as Lucas's mother, she wasn't going to give up until she had exhausted every single option.

MARTIN HAD GROWN UP hearing of the terrible fire in 1682 that had ruined the first Northfield Hall. His grandfather had shown him the smoke stains remaining on the ceiling of the dining room, in the only portion of the house that had survived, and told him of how proud the family was to have rebuilt an even better hall of England's finest red brick.

He had long ago accepted that his grandfather would disapprove of what Martin had done with the barony. But he wasn't prepared for how deeply he felt his grandfather's disappointment as he took in the ruins of Northfield Hall.

This house—the title—the family legacy—they had all been entrusted to him, and here was proof of what he had done with them: burned them to ash.

He slept for almost a full day in the Chows' cottage. Then he began his new life of wading through rubble in search of anything he could salvage. The first day, he found his steel safe tumbled out of its cupboard beside his desk. Though it was warped from heat, it still contained some banknotes, the family's royal letters patent, and the deed to the property. His desk was burnt down the middle, the contents of its drawers melted or fused or charred. All his wonderful bookshelves were reduced to stumps, the books transformed to black husks and ash.

The second day, Caroline helped him inspect the furniture that had been rounded up and laid in the cold December sun. His mother's rococo settees, ordered as a set from Paris, now stood on spindled legs empty of any upholstery. The long dining room table that his grandmother had commissioned when the Duke of Buckingham had come for a visit was now in three pieces, none of which could stand on their own. The mattresses were all burnt, the beds mangled from falling through the floors. Some things had survived: ivory chess pieces, the gilt frame of a looking glass, children's books and old journals that had been relegated to the upper stories.

Not enough.

Sophia arrived on the third day and joined Caroline, Eddie, and the household servants in collecting the shattered window glass. Eddie would melt it down in his workshop to reuse it. They filled a wagon hitched to the gig with the glass, but while Martin was trying to help, he sliced open his palm on a sharp edge, and he was told to spend the rest of the day supervising.

Nate joined them on the fourth day. Almost immediately, he turned into the naval captain he had once been and started organizing their haggard crew: the housemaids were sent to the barns to wash what had been saved while the footmen began dismantling what remained, salvaging every possible brick for reuse.

On the fifth day, Ellen appeared with a carriage full of supplies: clothes for Martin and the servants who lived in the Hall, burlap and tarps and axes for demolition, crates for storing what had been saved.

And on the sixth day, surprising everyone, arrived Benjamin and Lydia and the three little grandsons Martin had never before met. "We were coming for Christmas," Benjamin explained, "but now we are here to help."

By the seventh day, they had pulled down the charred staircase and half-standing walls. They stored bricks and wood and anything else that could be reused in the back of the barn with the cows, chickens, and goats. Soon, there would be nothing left to do except make plans for what came next. Martin needed to hire an architect to examine the foundation, which remained intact, and recommend how they rebuild. He also needed to find better lodgings for the household servants than the spare beds in cottages across the estate; he would have to remove himself from the Chows' soon, but he couldn't retreat to London when there was so much salvaging to be done. Could he bear to live in the White Hart for months on end?

Perhaps London was the best place for him. After all, this catastrophe was not some freak of nature: it was Martin's doing. His myopic, self-pitying doing.

As they rested for luncheon on the seventh day—the whole family huddling together in the dining hall along with the estate's laborers—Ellen said, "At least out of this disaster, we are all together. That is a blessing we can count, isn't it?"

Her siblings agreed cheerfully. This plunged Martin deeper into his brackish feelings, for after all, of all people, shouldn't *he* have been delighted to have all his children together, and to be sitting squished between the happy bodies of his four- and five-year-old grandsons?

None of his daughters had mentioned their last argument to him. He wondered if Caroline had told Nate—always her closest ally—that Martin had been misusing Martha. He suspected Sophia had told Benjamin about the will. Yet his children avoided any difficult subject, had not even asked him how the fire began, and it all made Martin feel so much worse. Clearly, they had no hope that they would get an honest answer from him. Or perhaps they had no intention of giving him their absolution. These topics were too dangerous because they were too hurtful, and so they must avoid them.

He wondered what Martha would think when she heard of the fire. She might have heard already: he had made Northfield Hall famous, sometimes infamous, in Britain, and the London newspapers must by now have the news of its ruin.

She, too, shouldn't forgive him, and so he hoped she would turn away from the news thinking, *He deserved it.*

Except he also couldn't help but want her to arrive in a carriage, just like his children had, and say, *You didn't deserve this.*

"I feel so silly. I'm sad as if someone died," Sophia said, "but it was only a building. I suppose I'm still grieving Uncle Maulvi."

Ellen put an arm around her sister. "It was more than a building. We all have so many memories there, and now we have lost it. You're not silly for feeling sad."

"I've seen sailors bawl when their ship was retired," Nate agreed. "It isn't a death, exactly, but certainly, we can never go back now."

"Nobody died," Martin heard himself say. He wished himself silent, but instead, he growled defensively: "Do not dishonor people who *have* died by comparing our loss of a fancy house with the loss of life."

Caroline glared at him. "None of us are saying it is the same thing. We are only saying we are sad. Is it dishonorable now to be sad?"

"No one was even injured." Thank God for that—Martin didn't know how he would face each day were he responsible for hurting someone.

"And that is a miracle, but it has no bearing on the fact that we lost our home."

Martin snarled: "Your home? As I recall, you abandoned it to live in Thatcham."

Caroline reared back to defend herself, but Ellen sliced a hand between them as if to break up a fight. "Really, Papa! There is no need to be churlish."

He could not refute the charge, but neither could he contain himself. On either side of him, Patrick and Rian leaned away, as if even they knew he was not to be trusted. Lydia took their hands and, making an excuse that they needed the privy, led them from the table.

Benjamin, the peacemaker, said, "It was a terrible accident, and Papa did the best he could. We can be very thankful that no one was injured, especially since it took so long to put out the fire."

"Yes, we can be," Ellen agreed, giving each of her siblings her "mother" look until they all nodded obediently. "And of all of us, Papa has lost the most. As he said, he is the only one of the family still living here."

"Then shouldn't he be mourning this accident with the rest of us, instead of making us feel like spoiled children?" Caroline said.

Nate and Sophia both tried to speak to reel her in, but Martin barely heard them. His heart was beating too fast as his mouth opened to say: "It wasn't an accident."

His children stared at him—and even though they each possessed individual faces and features, in that moment, they all looked exactly like Lolly. Softly, Benjamin repeated: "It wasn't an accident?"

"It was my fault."

"Your fault?" Caroline echoed, her voice sharp.

The confession was beginning to sting—a sting Martin deserved. He clarified: "I started it."

Sophia, gripping Caroline's hand, asked with all the disapproval of the governess she had once been, "Why would you start a fire?"

"I was burning letters. I poured my rum on the fire to make it hotter, and then the next thing I knew, it began spreading across the room." He looked at his fingers, pale and useless on the table. "I tried to stop it, but it spread so fast."

His children were so silent that the noise of the eating laborers—all those people who trusted him wrongly!—filled his ears.

"Where did you get rum?" Ellen asked. Her voice was as thin and desperate as it had been twelve years ago when she had discovered his scheme to sell Northfield Hall linens in London. After all, rum was a product of sugar plantations, and Martin had raised her to eschew anything touched by the sugar trade. "How often do you drink rum?"

"It was an old bottle from my father. I don't know why I saved it all these years. I never meant to drink it. Everyone had left. I've done everything wrong. So I decided I might as well drink it and burn all the letters...all the papers I didn't need anymore. I wanted to burn everything." He couldn't look at his children. "And that's what I ended up doing."

He awaited their judgment. It would be swift, he was sure. He had raised them to know right from wrong, and everything he had just confessed was wrong.

Would they banish him from the estate? Bar him from the London townhouse? Force him to beg the hospitality of one of his parliamentary allies?

Whatever they decided, Martin would abide it. After everything he had done, he could not earn back their trust, much less expect forgiveness. The only course available to him was to accept his punishment and hope it might reshape his character in however many years he had remaining in this life.

"But, Papa," Sophia said, "You didn't mean to. You didn't *intend* to burn down the house. You only meant to burn some papers."

Her eyes were so wide and uncertain, like when she had been a little girl asking why the stars only came out at night. Martin replied harshly, "What did I expect when I started throwing rum in the hearth?"

"You didn't expect this."

"Anyone could lose control of their fire," Ellen said. "It was an accident, Papa."

"An accident that wouldn't have happened if not for me." Martin didn't understand why this, of all his errors, they wanted to excuse.

"I shouldn't have been drunk. I shouldn't have been burning my letters. I shouldn't have been doing...any of the things I've been doing." He turned to Benjamin and Nate, who might have remained in ignorant bliss, and confessed: "I was carrying on an affair with Mrs. Bellamy while she stayed here. And I have written a will that leaves all my fortune to a trust for Northfield Hall, instead of any money going to you and your sisters. I have failed your sisters deeply. I have failed everyone deeply. I have been too wrapped up in my own ambitions to be a proper father or even a proper politician. And, my darlings—" His eyes fell on Ellen now, that first child who had taught him what it was to be a father, and her sisters beyond, and he remembered what it was like to hold them as infants, to offer their tiny fingers a grip as they learned to walk, to watch with worry as they grew into creatures that resembled adults. "I'm so sorry. I am sorry for every time I have failed you. I wish I could promise to do better, but it turns out everything I touch turns to ash."

All week long, he had managed to put one foot in front of the other by flogging himself with the evidence of what he had wrought. Suddenly, a wave of sorrow drowned his guilt and shame, and Martin could barely breathe for the pain.

Across the table, Caroline covered her mouth with her hand.

Ellen, rising from her place on the bench, came round the table and draped her warm arm across his back. "You raised us, Papa, and we are not ash."

"In spite of me," he said. "Sophia needed me, and I hardly even knew it! I should have ridden overnight through the rain to get to you. Why didn't I come when you asked me to?"

Sophia reached across the table and took one of his hands between her two soft palms. "I did not tell you how desperately I wanted your help."

"You were accused of a felony. You shouldn't have needed to tell me."

"And it injured me, Papa," she said, smiling, "but I did not turn to ash. You may make it up to me by forgiving yourself now, for I surely forgive you."

He clung to her hand, cherished Ellen's arm around him, and still did not believe he deserved them.

"Inspecting our recoveries yesterday, Mr. Chow pointed out a crate of things you rescued from the Hall yourself," Nate said. "I expected to find estate records or perhaps Mama's letters, but instead it was a rather surprising assortment from the garden drawing room."

"I only had time to fill my arms the once." Martin wished he could have saved Lolly's letters or the collection of illustrated books they had used to teach the children to read—or the entire Hall.

At least Martha's glove had been in his pocket, so he had not lost his only memento of her to his inferno.

"And you saved that terrible watercolor Sophia did of the pond?"

Martin squeezed that daughter's hand. "Who else would think to reflect the sunset in the pond by painting the water pink?"

"I am a visionary, Nathaniel," Sophia gloated.

"Yes, well, I can understand why you decided on the pens Ellen made you, but why keep the letter I wrote from Freetown about their record-keeping? That was surely the most boring thing I ever sent."

"It was the first one I received after almost a year of your letters being delayed on some ship that went off course. I had begun to worry you were dead." That episode of Martin's life—the months of wondering if he would ever hear of Nate, much less *from* him, again—was seared onto his heart, and he was surprised Nate didn't realize it. Until, of course, he reflected that he had never told Nate about it.

"We had all begun to worry," Caroline said, a little of the anger that she usually reserved for Martin now directed at her brother. "Most people who go to Sierra Leone die there."

"Yes, why should you be an exception?" Benjamin teased. Winking at his sister, he said, "Sophia had already begun forging your last will and testament so that she could receive whatever prize money you had earned."

"Well, here I am, alive and having forfeited the prize money as a disgraced officer."

"Did you save anything else, Papa?" Caroline asked, her eyes fixed on her plate.

Martin wondered what she hoped he had saved. Doubtless there were dozens of items from the Hall that she considered useful or important that he had left to the blaze. He had no option but to share the truth: "The portrait of Mama with you five, a book of Irish poetry that Benjamin once gifted me, and your essays."

"Did Benjamin write a good inscription for the poetry book at least, or is it only meaningful because you know it came from him?" Nate teased.

But Caroline literally elbowed her brother out of her way as she leaned forward to address Martin. "I didn't know you had my essays."

"Of course I do. You're a very fine writer." She had begun writing them the year of her marriage, and the next year published a collection with one of the radical Manchester presses.

Martin had ordered a hundred copies and stocked them in the London bookshops.

Perhaps he should have told Caroline, but she hadn't told *him* about the book, leaving him to find out from Ellen. Martin had been afraid Caroline would find fault with him for purchasing her essays, and so he had done it anonymously, just as she published them without her name.

But now he was confessing his crimes, he decided he might as well confess to this, too. "I am your distributor in London."

She paled, and Martin braced himself for the punishment he deserved. "*You* are? I thought it must be one of the printers, like Mr. Carlile. Why didn't you tell me?"

"I feared you would hate me for it."

"Why would I hate you for that?"

Martin felt that soul-piercing sorrow again. "You seem to hate everything I do."

When he looked at her, he saw his own pain mirrored in her eyes.

"I have failed you the most frequently and most deeply," he amended, "and I understand why you hate me. I hope you know that I *am* trying, Caro. I may never succeed, but I am trying to be the man you want me to be."

"I know," she said, and she looked down again.

Benjamin squeezed Martin's forearm. "You are being too harsh on yourself, Papa. To be human is to fail. You have failed while trying to be a good man. None of us fault you for that."

"I was not trying to be good when I started the fire. I was not trying to be good when I took up with Mrs. Bellamy." He was not trying to be good now, quarreling with his children instead of accepting their kindness.

"And what is this business with Mrs. Bellamy? Did you deceive her about your intentions?" Benjamin asked.

"No." He didn't think he could have deceived Martha if he had tried; she somehow knew his heart better than he did.

"Do you love her?" Ellen asked.

"It hardly matters after the way I...I sent her away."

"But do you love her?" Caroline asked, her voice soft.

He had lied about this before, even to himself, and he would have lied again, except sometime in the course of this confession, his heart had broken free of its cage. "Yes, I do."

Ellen's arm around his shoulders tightened. Sophia's palms around his hand squeezed. Benjamin's hand on his forearm gripped more firmly. Nate let out a sigh. And across the table, Caroline's eyes shone. "That's all that matters, Papa. I know we are supposed to learn from you, but haven't you learned anything about love from us?"

"We've each chosen love, after all, and I'd say it has worked out," Nate added.

"Aren't you proud of us?" Sophia asked.

"Aren't you happy for us?" Benjamin said.

He was. Of course he was. Did they even need to ask?

"You needn't cling to Mama's memory," Ellen said. "If you want to marry again, you should."

"She is a clergyman's widow."

"And therefore she is not the right class?" Caroline cried.

Martin remembered Martha on the gig beside him, letting him parse his complicated thoughts on the order of their society. And how natural it had felt whenever she sat with him in his study, going over work for the estate. And that memory from the carriage he had promised to keep forever, when they had been nothing but two people in giddy lust for each other.

He answered Caroline: "Therefore, I would be a hypocrite to wed her when I tried to stop you from marrying Eddie."

Caroline covered her face with her hands. For a moment, Martin thought that was the only reaction he would earn from her—and was it anger? Dismay? Sorrow? He didn't know.

Then she said, "Papa, you have hurt me, and I have hurt you, and it has all spilled into hurting everyone."

Martin wished he could take her in his arms. "All I ever want is to do right by you."

"Then go tell Mrs. Bellamy you love her. Be honest—to yourself, to us, to the world. That's all I've ever wanted from you."

Be honest. Tell Martha he loved her. Confess to *her* all he had done.

Martin didn't know if he had the heart for it, but, with his children embracing him, he resolved to try.

Chapter Nineteen

I N A WAY, MARTHA did not mind that her quest extended across days. So long as she did not find Lucas's grave, she still had a reason to venture out of the boarding house. She did most of her searching in the afternoons and evenings, though her landlady continuously admonished her for staying out after dark. "Take the wrong turn," warned the woman, "and you'll end up with the molls on Avon Street."

"I hardly think anyone would pay for my wares," Martha replied on receiving this warning the fifth day in a row, which succeeded in leaving the landlady flabbergasted but did not prevent her the following morning from advising Martha to return before three.

In fact, as her search went on, the early evenings helped Martha. She had begun in the newspaper office, searching through their archives to see if Lucas's burial had been mentioned in the death announcements—and indeed, she found it. On April 30, 1812, a brief paragraph read:

On Saturday last, a man from Tolpuddle retired to his room and shot himself in bed. The coroner has ruled it "felo de se" and he has been buried at a crossroads near town.

But all of this, Martha had already known. She wondered if this very newspaper article had been delivered to her and Kenneth by whoever had told them the news. She couldn't now remember *how* they had found out. Someone had ridden to Tolpuddle from Bath—perhaps a curate sent by a sympathetic rector? Or had it been Lady Imogen's father, who had seemed to have friends keeping an eye on his daughter while she lived?

Either way, the newspaper did not answer the question of where Lucas was buried. The clerk who minded the archives helpfully introduced Martha to the two reporters who wrote the bulk of the articles, but neither of them had been with the paper in 1812, nor did they think the writer would know which crossroads were referenced. "We don't ask for many details about that sort of thing," the senior reporter explained, "unless the deceased is a person of import."

Lucas, of course, had only been a person of import to *her*. Martha squared her shoulders. "If it were a person of import, how would you go about finding out?"

"I suppose I'd try to find one of the gravediggers."

And so Martha set off in search of the men who might have dug Lucas's grave. Bath had dozens of churches from which they might have been hired; after spending a day asking deacon after deacon whether they could direct her to gravediggers, she concluded she was most likely to find the men in question at the Griffin Inn on Milk Street.

A public house was no place for an old woman, but she compromised with herself by going as the sun set around four and staying only until seven or eight. The first night, she drank two pints of lager and heard the confession of a young man about how much he missed his grandmother. The second night, she had a third lager to stay in conversation with a man who dug graves for the Catholic cemetery, but he didn't know anything about suicides and had only come to Bath three years before. At last, on a Saturday night, she stayed long enough that a crew of gravediggers came in after finishing a funeral for St. Swithin's. The publican, who had decided she was his responsibility, introduced her. "Any of you lads digging graves back in '12?"

Two of them had been. They were middle-aged men, one with a permanent sunburn and the other swarthy, and they looked at her with a certain weariness. "I'm trying to find where my son was buried," she explained. The story was growing easier to tell now that she had stopped trying to pretend it wasn't so. "He died by his own hand, and all they said was a crossroads near town."

The sunburned man said, "We bury more of those than you might think."

"Do you always use the same crossroads?"

He shook his head. "Was he young?"

"Twenty-two. He had eloped here with an earl's daughter. They were happy, I think, but she died in childbirth, and that's when he..."

"The Earl of Lygon?" asked the swarthy man.

Hope flared in her heart. "That's right."

"At a lodging house on Corn Street?"

"Yes, that's where Lucas lived."

He nodded sadly. "One of the earl's men came to supervise us, which is why I remember it. Your Lucas is buried at the crossroads of Lansdown Road and Charlcombe Lane. On the northern side by a silver birch tree."

Martha had always imagined Lucas's body directly beneath the road—but of course, it would be too disruptive to traffic to turn up the dirt whenever a *felo de se* needed burial. Now, she pictured a birch tree, firm but slender, too tall to cower in the wind, and she felt a surprising surge of joy.

At last, she knew where to find her child.

On Sunday, she attended the early service at the chapel near Seymour Street. Then, wearing her full mourning outfit, she walked up Lansdown Road. It was a long walk: through the Upper Town, past elegant Camden Crescent, and up the slope of the hill. She relished the ache in her legs and the burning of her lungs, for this was a pilgrimage. She paused now and then to sip water but never to look back. She would not think of what awaited her when she had finished this quest. She would only focus on Lucas, waiting for her under a silver birch.

At last, after the sun had already reached its peak, Martha found the crossroads with Charlcombe Lane. On the north side, just as the gravedigger promised, was a silver birch tree, upright and proud even in the cold afternoon wind. The ground beneath it was covered in yellowed grass. Martha took off her gloves and touched first the trunk of the tree, then the ground beneath it, with her bare fingers.

"My darling Lucas, I'm sorry it took me so long to find you. I'm sorry it took me so long to forgive you."

Sinking against the tree, Martha shut her eyes and, fingers still clinging to the grass, murmured the prayers she used to say with Lucas when putting her boy to bed. She prayed for God to look after him, even though she knew Kenneth taught that there was no place for a soul like Lucas's in Heaven. She prayed for Lucas to forgive her and for him to somehow, wherever he was, take strength from how much she loved him.

Loved him—and admired him for being brave, even though it had led him to disaster. Lucas had not taken what she and Kenneth told him life offered. He had refused to let others limit his potential. He had followed his heart, and if the rest of the world were as brave as him, then he and Lady Imogen should have had every reason to expect happiness.

Martha knew now the freedom that came from confessing love, even when it wasn't meant to be, and she was proud Lucas had shown the courage to be true to Lady Imogen no matter the consequences.

Opening her eyes, Martha took in the vista that was Lucas's dominion. The birch tree was at a curve of Lansdown Hill, which meant that all of Bath was spread below. She could see the glimmering white buildings of Upper Town, the squares and crescents laid out as if she were examining a map, the River Avon cutting like a blue sash across a maiden's gown. It was a prospect worth paying for, and Lucas had it for all eternity.

"Do you forgive me, Lucas?" she asked aloud.

In response, the wind stilled and the sun, peeking out from between clouds, shone directly on her.

And suddenly she was lighter than she had been in years. She had still lost Lucas—that loss she would never forget—but Martha no longer felt his fist around her heart, dragging her down.

They had forgiven each other; they loved each other; they must both move on.

"What shall I do next?" she asked, but this time, she got no elemental response.

She supposed she could establish herself in Bath. With Lord Preston's money, she had enough to rent more permanent rooms. She could take the waters, as one was supposed to do in Bath, and play cards with other widows and visit Lucas every week. Perhaps she would even meet another man to love and cherish, one who was kind like Lord Preston but appropriate like Kenneth.

She could also still go live with Georgina. She could rent a room in London. She could go to the Continent! She could go anywhere, do anything, that would not drain her one hundred pounds (now ninety-eight pounds) too quickly.

The one thing she could not do was return to Northfield Hall.

From that weight—heartbreak—she was not yet free. Yet Martha knew that if she waited long enough, and if she designed a firm enough life for herself, one day she would be sitting on a different hill, touched by a different breeze, and discover she no longer mourned the love she might have had with Lord Preston.

Until then, she resolved to live the best life available to her.

It was as she deliberated what "best" might mean to her that she heard the thud of hoofbeats climbing Lansdown Road. She shrank against the silver birch, determined not to be moved no matter who the stranger was, and so it took her a few moments to recognize the rider quickly approaching:

Lord Martin Preston.

CHAPTER TWENTY

F INDING MARTHA HAD NOT been as simple as traveling to her niece's address in London. Firstly because Martin didn't have the niece's address, though a letter for Martha, sans return address, did at last arrive at Northfield. He began by asking Reading Savings Bank if she had cashed his banknote; this was when he discovered she was in Bath, not London. Getting to Bath was easy enough, but her bank was less forthcoming in disclosing her lodgings, and so Martin spent Saturday discreetly inquiring at the Pump Room, the Cross Bath, and the Assembly Hall if anyone had made the acquaintance of Mrs. Bellamy—claiming he had family news he needed to share.

A few people had heard of the fire at Northfield Hall and wanted him to tell it in gory detail, but none of them knew of a recently arrived widow from Berkshire.

On Sunday, he had Boyle begin knocking at lodging houses. He was lucky to guess correctly that she might choose Seymour Street—a modest neighborhood—over the fashionable Sydney Place, and on the fourth door, they found her landlady, a middle-aged woman who clearly knew the entire street's business.

"She *said* she was going to climb to Lansdown Road and Charlcombe Lane, but there is no good reason for a body to do that, so I suspect you'll find her somewhere near Camden Crescent."

Martin was too relieved to have found her to realize the significance of a crossroads. He directed Boyle back to his coaching inn and hired a stallion. Knowing that Martha was alone, he did not want to execute the rest of his mission in the company of Boyle. He carried with him the various tokens of apology he had gathered along the way: her niece's letter; the lace glove she had left behind at Northfield Hall; a book by Thomas Paine, which he'd bought from a bookseller in Bath yesterday after he could not find her.

Martin wasn't quite sure what he was going to say to her when he found her. No explanation would erase the pain he had caused her, nor any apology give her reason to trust him with her heart again.

He could only hope that her mercy was greater than his failures.

By the time the stallion carried him to the top of the hill, Martin was stiff with nerves. He worried he had missed Martha, or perhaps the landlady had been wrong—but then he spotted her. A silver-haired woman dressed all in black, sitting against the trunk of a tree.

She turned her head to watch him approach, but she did not rise from the ground. Martin slowed his stallion, dismounted, and tied the horse to a fencepost out of kicking range of the birch tree.

"What are you doing here?" Martha asked in the careful, emotionless tone she had used in all their early conversations.

"Your landlady said I would find you here." He waited for his heart, which was beating triple time, to deliver him the words that would make everything right. He looked at the dirt crossroads and realized the heaviness of where he stood. "Is this where Lucas is buried?"

She nodded.

"Is that why you came to Bath?"

"I needed to say goodbye." She leaned her head against the tree trunk, eyes closed, and Martin's heart twisted at her burden. A mother should never have to bury her child; if she did have to, she should not have to chase down his grave a decade later. "I needed him to forgive me."

"Forgive you?" They had bonded over this before, yet, with his children's blessings filling his heart, Martin suddenly saw it in a new light. Martha had done no worse by Lucas than he had done by Caroline, and that was to make honest mistakes. "For loving him as best you could as his mother? For trying to protect him?"

"He didn't come to me for support—for money or for his grief—because I was always too busy telling him the right thing to do. Experience told him that my advice, if I even dared to see him, would only make things worse." Eyes still closed, she pressed her hands to her heart. "And I think he was right."

Martin didn't agree. Had her son come to her in despair, he knew Martha would have reacted with wisdom and care. But this was not about arguing the point. He asked, "Has he forgiven you, then?"

At last, her eyes opened, and she smiled beatifically at the landscape beyond. "Yes, I think so."

He sank onto the ground beside her. "Tell me about him."

"He was a feeling kind of boy," Martha said, running her fingers over the yellowed grass under which Lucas might now be resting. "When he was five, I lost a baby, and he understood enough to know that I was upset, even though I tried not to let him see me ill or crying. He made me a little doll out of straw to cheer me up."

"That's a good heart."

"He looked out for others, too, not just me. One of his best friends broke his ankle, and Lucas spent every afternoon inside keeping him company, even on the most beautiful summer afternoons. He always put others first."

Martin watched her whole countenance brighten even as tears shone in her eyes. Wanting to see more of this, he asked, "And did he never make mischief?"

"Oh, he knew how to get my hackles up, that's for sure. Every time I made him a new suit of clothes—every time, I swear!—he managed to tear it or roll around in mud or otherwise ruin it within the first two days. He must have been sixteen the time that we purchased him a proper coat from a shop in town, so he could be proud at school, and that very afternoon, he somehow ended up in the river. He was wet from head to toe."

Martin smiled because she was smiling. "I'll never stop being amazed at how young people can speak and look like adults only to behave like the littlest of children."

"Lucas was like that. Sometimes, he said the wisest things to me. Other times, he did the most harebrained things." Her gaze drifted over the crossroads. "I was never sympathetic to him falling in love with Lady Imogen. I told him to keep his eyes off her; he didn't listen. I told him not to go following her around the countryside; he didn't listen. I told him he would never be allowed to marry her; he told me I could never understand him. When they eloped, and when he...it is only since I have fallen in love with you that I understand why he couldn't see reason. He was young. What match was he for the power of the heart?"

Martin knew this moment was not about him. Yet he heard her confession—*I have fallen in love with you*—and all the fears and shadows that had been weighing him down disappeared. He had been afraid her heart had already released him. He couldn't help but sweep Martha's beautiful hands into his. "We are old, and what match are we for the power of our hearts?"

She looked at him with that shield over her emotions again. "Why have you come after me, Lord Preston?"

He had too many apologies to make. He didn't know where to start. When he opened his mouth, none of them came out. "I came to tell you that I am in love with you, too."

She softened only a little. "This is a long journey to make just to say such a thing."

"It is no small thing to say." Martin dared kiss the tips of her fingers, which she hadn't yet pulled from his clasp. "If that is all you want to hear from me, then I will return home knowing that at least you know the truth of my heart."

Martha whispered, "And if I want to hear more from you?"

"Then I shall tell you that I am so deeply sorry for how I treated you. All this time, we called ourselves friends, and I was afraid to admit that we were more than friends because I could not bear to wonder what a future might hold for us. Now I have seen what a future is *without* you, and I hate it. I am at my worst without you." He forced himself to not look away as he confessed: "I burned down Northfield Hall."

"Burned it down?" She jerked forward. "Not the whole building, surely? How? Is everyone all right?"

Before his admission to his children, Martin would have absorbed her questions as accusations. Now, he refused to let guilt sink its claws into his heart. He would be honest; no more, no less. "Luckily, no one was injured, but I'm afraid the whole building burned. I had too much to drink, and the fire in the hearth got out of control."

He would not shrink away from her, not even as she frowned. "That doesn't sound like you."

"And yet, it was me. My fault. My actions." Martin's heart was beating in triple time again. "That is who I became when I tried so very hard to deny that I am a man with a heart. A heart that, at the time, was in great pain."

Her eyes cast down as she said sympathetically, "Grief makes us do strange things."

"Yes, and I have been grieving a great many things. Mr. Maulvi. My good relationship with my children. You. But do you know, it is Caroline who prodded me into realizing that I needn't grieve you at all." Martin dared to hold her hand a little more tightly. "You have been the best partner to me, Martha. I was ashamed of all the wrong things. I should never have sent you away. I should have begged you to stay. I don't deserve your forgiveness, but I humble myself with the apology because at the very least, you deserve to know that I repent every injury I caused you."

Martha's fingers began to tremble. "You are worthy of forgiveness."

He remembered her last words to him: *It doesn't do any good when you are so hard on yourself.* "My son Benjamin recently informed me that I am human, and therefore I inevitably will fail. Which is very similar to advice Maulvi used to give me, and perhaps even what Lolly used to remind me of all those years ago."

"That you expect too much of yourself?"

"That trying not to do something wrong often leads to not doing the right thing." Martin kissed her fingertips again. "In this case, I know the right thing is confessing my love for you. From there, I have some ideas, but it does depend on what you want."

Martha whispered, "I never asked for anything from you, Lord Preston."

He reached for her chin, pulling her close. "Perhaps you should. Perhaps you should demand to call me Martin."

"Let me call you anything I want," she breathed in reply.

"Fine, you may call me by any name. What else? Would you like me to leave you in peace?"

She shook her head, touching the tip of her nose to his. "No, I want you to stay."

"Would you like me to marry you?"

Her breath stopped for a moment. "What would people say if *I* were to be Lady Preston?"

"My children are very much in favor of the idea, and based on Boyle's enthusiasm for helping me find you, I gather the rest of the neighborhood would make no complaints."

He could hear hope in how she swallowed. "What of London society?"

"They will have opinions, as they always do, but theirs are easy for me to ignore." Bringing her hands to press against his chest, Martin said, "I am not sure I deserve you, Martha Bellamy, but I love your character, I love your body, and I love the partnership we found with each other. If you so desire it, I beg you, will you make me the happiest man and marry me?"

Martha was almost smiling. "Yes, I shall." She leaned in so her lips hovered beyond his. "It is, according to my son, what two people do when they fall in love."

"I think Lucas had that right." Martin cradled her cheeks, savoring this woman who was such a surprising gift, before taking the kiss he had longed for since the moment he reached the crossroads.

THEY WALKED BACK TO Bath hand in hand. Lord Preston led the horse by its reins, and when the road narrowed, he let Martha step ahead so they could go single file. Martha tried to accustom herself to calling him "Martin," but he had been "Lord Preston" in her mind for so long that she wasn't sure she could make the adjustment. She supposed he would marry her either way.

Marriage. As they ambled down the hill, Martha turned the idea over in her head, a little afraid of how giddy it made her. She had pictured marriage to Lord Martin Preston in her wildest moments at Northfield Hall—mostly in the aftermath of their lovemaking, when he curled around her for a snooze—but she had never considered it a practical possibility. She was too common, too old, and still in mourning for her first husband.

Now here she was, holding his hand in public. Every now and then, as they discussed the ruin of Northfield Hall, Martin's words dried up so that he could smile at her, and then she couldn't help but smile at him, and once they nearly walked off the road because they were so busy grinning about the future that lay ahead of them.

It would not be a simple future, and not just because they were of different classes. The family home was reduced to ashes, and it was not as easy as rebuilding what had previously been there. Lord Preston—Martin—faced a hundred decisions, big and small, in remaking Northfield Hall. "They are our decisions to make together," he said, smiling at her, as he summed up his main concerns. "If they don't scare you away, that is."

"On the contrary. As you said, we make a good partnership." Martha saw the opportunity for what it was: a chance for everyone to start anew. The old Northfield Hall had been a relic, and the new one would reinvigorate Martin's vision for the estate, for his family—and for their marriage, where Martha would no longer have to fit into the boxed rooms of Martin's established life. "Is Benjamin staying on as steward?"

"He and Lydia and the boys will remain until the summer, but then he is determined to return to his property in Ireland. He says it needs him more than Northfield Hall needs him." For once, Martin didn't look pained as he talked about a child wandering away from him. "He is doing good work there."

"He is following in his father's footsteps."

"Doing better than his father." Martin smiled. "However, now, among everything else, I must hire a steward who knows enough to be useful but will not impede the mission of Northfield."

"Perhaps you need look no farther than Northfield Hall to find such a person."

He looked at her as if such an idea had never occurred to him—and as if it were instantly blossoming into a hundred new ideas. Martha couldn't help but giggle at this man who was so dear and so brilliant.

And now hers!

Martin kissed her fingertips again. "Oh, I have been remiss in giving you a letter that arrived from your niece." He gestured at his coat pocket, so Martha helped herself to the letter.

It was a small piece of paper with not too many words. Bracing herself, Martha opened it, prepared to hear that Georgina did not have the heart to take in her poor, widowed aunt.

Instead, it was an invitation to come stay for as long as she needed.

"She says she has set aside a room for me close enough to the hearth that I won't get cold in the winter."

Martin raised an eyebrow. "Then you needn't marry me out of desperation."

"Quite. I suppose I shall pack my bags for Battersea," she teased.

He tugged her close. "I would follow you and beg you to marry me until you finally said yes."

"My love for a niece can never be replaced by my love for a man."

"I shall live in your room near the hearth so you are never torn asunder from dear Georgina."

"Now *that* is true love." Martha couldn't bear teasing any longer. She just wanted to beam at him.

Martin beamed back. "How would you like to be married? I could arrange a special license so that we could marry here in Bath within the week. Or we could return to Thatcham and have the banns called."

"I want to marry at Northfield, and I want all your children to be there, if they are willing." She brushed the skirt of her stiff bombazine mourning gown. "However, it is still two months until I am done mourning Kenneth."

Though Martin nodded to acknowledge the point, he said softly, "Mourning never truly ends."

It was her turn to kiss his fingertips, for with that one sentence she knew they did not need a protracted conversation about whether part of their hearts would remain allied with their lost spouses. "All the same, I would prefer not to marry you in my widow's weeds."

"What do you propose?"

"Let me remain here in Bath for the winter. I shall finish my period of mourning, arrange a new wardrobe, and do all the other things a bride is supposed to do to prepare for her marriage. When the roads clear in the springtime, I shall return to Thatcham, and we can be married at Northfield."

Even though they were approaching Bath proper now and there were more people around, Martin stopped where he was and pulled Martha close to his body. "That's months apart from each other."

"But then we'll have the rest of our lives together. And we won't have started our marriage in a cradle of gossip."

There would still be some talk in Thatcham, of course, and the London papers would drum up all sorts of scandals to explain why a baron decided to marry a matronly widow. But at least no one could say that Martha was disrespecting Kenneth; at least no one could point to an obvious sign that Lord Preston might have taken advantage of her.

"I shall miss you terribly," he growled.

She smirked, her eyes on those lips of his that tantalized her so. "Is that a promise?"

"It is a certainty. I would kiss you right here on the street to prove it if you weren't concerned about gossip."

Martha took his lapels in either hand. "Gossip in Bath won't hurt us." Stretching onto her toes, she kissed him. Briefly—but deeply. She could feel his body stir and might have kept teasing him with her tongue if someone passing by hadn't cried out,

"I say!"

Martin withdrew, his eyes hazy. "I suppose I should take you back to Seymour Street."

She smirked again. "I would rather see your rooms."

And so they guided the stallion back to York House. Giving Martha directions to his room, Martin took the horse to its stable, and Martha slipped upstairs without earning so much as a second glance. By the time Martin tapped on the door with their secret knock, she had undressed to just her petticoat, stays, and stockings, her hair let loose from its braid. She lay down on the mattress before calling out, "Enter."

He stood for a moment by the door, eyes sweeping over her, and she watched a deep pink work its way up his skin. "My dear Martha," he said, breath shaking, and then he all but leapt upon her.

They had a lot of kissing to make up for. For a long while, that was all they did. Deep, languid kisses that could have lasted all afternoon. Martin's hands curled through her hair and strayed down to her waist, and Martha palmed the muscular arms and chest she had so missed these past weeks, but they remained in the fuzzy simplicity of the kiss for far longer than they had ever permitted themselves before. By the time Martin leaned back, Martha's body felt soft and warm and liquid.

He reached into his pocket—for he was still wearing all his clothes!—and withdrew a lace glove. "I found this under your bed after you left. I have to admit, I've grown very fond of it, but I suppose you might want it back."

It was from her fancy set of gloves, which were made of lace and ended just before the tip of each finger, serving as adornment rather than providing warmth. Martha had not mourned the lost glove deeply—though she had saved its forlorn mate in her sewing kit—but she was almost overwhelmed with joy at seeing it in Martin's hand. Taking it, she slipped it over her fingers and held it up for display. "I thought the poor thing was lost forever."

Martin seized her wrist, his eyes nearly black with desire. "I want to see you wearing nothing except this glove."

Her body nearly rippled with a sensual thrill. She demanded more. "What will you do with me when this is all I wear?"

He knew what she wanted—and he gave it to her, curving over her to growl in her ear, "I am going to shag you so hard you won't remember your name. I'm going to make your cunt as wet as a fountain. I'm going to fill you with my roger and rut you senseless."

It was all Martha could do to see straight after that. She stripped naked, as requested. Martin removed his clothes in a rush, too. When his cock stood free and proud from his trousers, Martha pumped it with her gloved hand, just to see how deep a groan she could pull from him.

From the sound of it, he was either in mortal pain or the most excruciating pleasure of his life.

"Let me work your cunny the way it deserves," he growled, taking her hips to position her on her knees. Then, reaching from behind, he worked her quim with his fingers and thumb until she could feel the froth of desire threatening to drip from the mattress. "No pomade required today," he said, voice thick with satisfaction. "Are you ready for me to take you as my betrothed?"

"I'll tell you if we're betrothed once you've proven you can swive me with your prick," Martha teased back. He groaned again, this time almost directly into her ear. Then he thrust inside of her, his thighs against the backs of her legs, his thumb still teasing her quim's peak.

It was all Martha had ever fantasized about. A forbidden fuck riddled with forbidden words with the safest man in the world. She had craved Martin for weeks, had been beside him for hours, had kissed him for minutes, and it took only the sweetest amount of time for her body to shatter into the deepest orgasm of her life. Martin rode the wave with her, his torso curling over hers, and they fell, spent, to the mattress still joined at the hip.

"My Martha. My love," Martin murmured into her ear.

And at last, she truly did believe she was his beloved. She smiled back at him. "Yes, I think I'll marry you after all."

Chapter Twenty One

April 1824

Over the decades, Northfield had hosted dozens of weddings. The first Martin remembered was his own to Lolly thirty-six years ago. He could still recall the dizzying glory of holding her hands, the heady relief of finding a partner to share his lot in life, the smell of lilacs in the air as they vowed to usher in a new era for Northfield and everyone who lived there.

Since then, he had celebrated the marriages of farmhands, carpenters, gardeners, housemaids, butlers, weavers, and three of his children. Martin had walked brides to the dais, stood up with grooms, made speeches on the couple's merits, retired to his suite to admire the revelry from afar.

This was the first wedding since the fire. It was the first celebration of any kind without the great house. It turned out they had never needed the Hall for their celebrations. Instead of readying himself in the calm of his private sitting room, Martin dressed at the Chows' cottage, which he had been calling home these past four months. He waited for the festivities to begin with Benjamin and Nate in the brewery, listening to his sons banter as his heart beat fast in anticipation of the event. Martha, wonderful Martha, waited nearby in the dining hall, and everyone else gathered on the ghostly outline of what had once been the great house.

In the summer, construction would begin on new buildings, which would include a modest house for the family and a community hall to provide a library, classrooms, reading rooms, and more. For the moment, the old footprint of the Hall blurred with wedding decorations. The dais stood on the scarred ground of the garden drawing room. The spectators—Martin's family, Martha's niece, everyone from Northfield, almost all of Thatcham, even a few dignified visitors from London—congregated where previously the corridor had connected the rooms, and benches and tables awaited their feast on the earth where once Martin's study and foyer and dining rooms had stood.

The air began to buzz with conversation as the crowd awaited the ceremony. Martin resisted the urge to loosen his cravat. He was anxious, not about marrying Martha, but about their duty to this crowd afterward.

The ceremony took place on the dais erected by the Chow family. Mr. Sebright conducted the vows without any invectives, thanks to Martin's generous purchase of new pews for the parish church.

Martha, wearing a simple green gown to match the springtime buds, beamed at Martin as she said her vows. As for him, he had to focus on the feel of her lace gloves that didn't quite reach her fingertips, or else he would have teared up as he promised to cherish her for as long as they both should live.

And then they were married. Husband and wife, in a sacred union, never to be torn asunder.

The crowd cheered, and Martin kissed Martha on the lips, forgetting for once his obligation to decorum.

And then it was time for a Northfield feast: steamed buns, hand pies, and fried fish. Every person helped themselves from the buffet, and they sat not according to a seating chart but according to affinity.

Martin and Martha took a table in the center, just about where the foyer staircase used to stand. His children quickly filled in around him: Nate and Amy to his left, Sophia and John across the bench, beside them Caroline and Eddie and two-month-old Thomas Paine Chow. One table over, Ellen and Max and their five children occupied a bench while Benjamin and Lydia and their three children sat opposite.

Martha's niece, Georgina, and her brood sat nearby, too. As one of the children exclaimed about the food, Martha leaned in to murmur, "I'm so happy that it is beginning to feel wicked."

Martin wrapped his arm around her waist, which was restrained considering he wanted to tackle her to the ground and cover her in kisses. "I'll show you wickedness, madam, just you wait."

"I grow impatient," she teased back. Her words were hardly louder than a breath, but Sophia interrupted:

"If you two are going to be so indecent, John and I will be, too." She made as if to climb onto her husband's lap—and John made as if to permit it.

"You'll wake the baby!" Caroline protested, poking her sister back onto the bench.

They were saved from further hijinks by Mr. Chow climbing the dais to make a toast. "Lord Preston, there is one thing that unites almost everyone here. In our hour of need, you welcomed us into your home. For too many years, you stood alone between us and the harsh winds of the wider world. Our hearts are gladdened to see you with a new lady love. May you and Lady Preston find great happiness together!"

Martha blushed beautifully at her new title. Martin couldn't help but press a kiss to her cheek, as if to pin that blush in place.

The Widow Croft took the dais next. "I am here to speak for both myself and my sweet, lately departed Mr. Maulvi. For his part, Mr. Maulvi considered Lord Preston his dearest friend in the world. I believe that he had an inkling of what was in Lord Preston's heart towards the new Lady Preston, and I know that from wherever he is now, he blesses this marriage. For my part, those of us from Thatcham can tell you there is no greater woman than Lady Preston. When you need help, she is there. No wonder she and his lordship have found a love match when their hearts are made from the same mold. May you have health and happiness for many years to come!"

Martin and Martha sipped their elder wine in response to the hearty cheer this earned. He looked around the tables, wondering how everyone would react when they discovered what he and Martha had planned for them.

Perhaps Martha could read his mind: she leaned in to ask, "Would you like to announce your news now?"

They had debated whether to make the announcement on their wedding day or wait until the spring planting was done. After consulting with his children, however, Martin and Martha had agreed it was best to do it while everyone was gathered—and already feeling happy about the future.

Before Martin could rise from his seat, however, Benjamin and Caroline took the stage. "We would like to say a few words on behalf of our family," Benjamin began, his practiced voice booming across the crowd. "I must admit, when Papa first confessed to us his intentions towards our new stepmother, I was shocked. I forgot my father is also a man who needs—and deserves—a partner in life, just like anyone else. However, this confession came in the wake of the fire that claimed Northfield Hall, which showed me the great beauty of how in our worst moments, we can also see more clearly what truly matters to us. For my father, that is having the woman he loves by his side."

Caroline added: "Papa, we would like you to know that we five—and your nine grandchildren—love you with all of our hearts. You are our bulwark, and when we have quarreled, it is only because we always assumed you were more god than man. I am so glad that you have found happiness with the new Lady Preston. When I see you together, I see a fuller version of you. I am proud to be your daughter, and I am proud to call the new Lady Preston my stepmother."

As everyone around him raised their glasses in cheers, Martin found himself frozen, paralyzed by the relief he felt to hear those words from Caroline.

Martha whispered in his ear, "It's true, you know. She *is* proud to be your daughter."

"She is even more proud to call you her stepmother," he replied, stealing Martha's fingertips for a kiss. "Will you come with me to make our announcement?"

She nodded, excitement glowing in her eyes. "Let me say the part about Caroline."

Together, they walked to the dais. From the tables came cheers and a few bawdy jokes. Martin acknowledged it all with a wave; Martha smiled shyly at the group of two hundred or so people gathered before them.

She surprised him by speaking first. "Thank you all for coming to celebrate with us. I did not know what kind of reception to expect when Lord Preston did me the great honor of proposing marriage, and I am truly humbled to know that we are all part of the same community forever after."

This was met with a cheer, and several people tipped back their glasses in approval.

"It is important to know that what my *husband*—" Martha emphasized the word by turning to grin at Martin "—is about to announce comes from years of great ruminations. I may have suggested some practicalities, but you must trust that any changes come from his wisdom and vision of a Northfield that continues to be a haven for all."

Martin wouldn't have phrased it so ominously. A pall descended as everyone—even his children, who already knew what he would say—tensed. Squeezing Martha's hand, Martin took up his part of the speech.

"For a long time now, I have pondered how to ensure that the legacy of Northfield can sustain every newcomer who needs our welcome and every family that wants to remain here for generations. It is a question of money as well as natural resources, and balancing the demands of the here and now versus the greater good. Traditionally, these decisions have landed on the shoulders of the Baron Ashforth, whoever he may be. However, it is time for that tradition, like many others we have changed, to transform."

Taking a deep breath, Martin gestured to the gaping landscape around them where once had stood the great house. "Just as we are going to rebuild a Hall that serves everyone, not only the baron's family, so will we change our decision-making processes to include everyone's voice. Instead of hiring a new steward to do my bidding, we are establishing a stewardship council to oversee the care and funds of Northfield. There will be one representative for every fifty adults who have lived at Northfield for at least one year, as well as a representative of the Preston family, and the representatives will be elected every five years. We will hold our first elections by secret ballot on the summer solstice, and I invite every eligible adult—man *and* woman—to consider whether they should like to run for this solemn duty."

As these words rang out, Martin felt a great calm settle in his bones. Here he was, holding Martha's hand, bathed in spring sunshine, and for the first time in his life, caring for two hundred people did not weigh on him like a hundred-pound stone.

"In fact, we are pleased to announce that for the council's first term, the family has elected Mrs. Caroline Chow as our representative," Martha said, beaming like a proud mother.

Caroline stood to accept the round of applause.

"Today is a day of celebration. Lady Preston and I wanted you to know that just as our marriage is the beginning of something new for us, it is also the beginning of something new for Northfield—something that I hope you will join me in considering an improvement for everyone. Now, please, raise your cups once more to toast my wonderful bride, family, and this singular community!"

This earned him the heartiest cheers yet. Fueled by the crowd's enthusiasm—and his own relief—Martin could no longer keep his impulses in check. Right there on the dais, he pulled Martha into his arms and claimed a great and wonderful kiss.

His wife, his partner, his inspiration. Soon, they would head to London for the parliamentary season, which meant a new set of challenges and moral quandaries as they continued his fight against imperial injustices. Too, they would guide the stewardship council, especially in its first few years. And there would be their own relationship to navigate amidst decisions about the new Hall and negotiations about which balls to attend and disagreements over things small and large.

He looked forward to all of it. He wanted to miss none of it. He had Martha, he had his children, he had a new Northfield and all the old problems that Britain still hadn't conquered.

In the meantime, he would embarrass her with the strength of his affection.

To a chorus of whoops, Martha pushed away, joking, "When does our honeymoon begin?"

He laughed because he wouldn't mind that himself. But neither did he want to leave this beautiful afternoon, surrounded by everyone he held dear. Clinging to Martha, he returned to their table.

"I think it's a stunning idea, Papa," Ellen said from the next bench. "I'm glad you are brave enough to give it a try."

He had discussed it with his children when they had all arrived the previous week, and they had stood as witnesses to his new will, which directed all his money except Lolly's dowry to be established in a Northfield trust.

Her husband Max grinned. "If it's a success, we might steal it in a few years for Hope Hall."

"*Might*?" Ellen raised a brow at her husband, and Martin could see a lively debate sparking between them.

"The London papers will be calling you a seditionist by tomorrow morning," said Benjamin. "Which only means it is the obviously right thing to do."

Lydia said wistfully, "I think the idea would take on like wildfire in Ireland. All anyone wants is a say in how things are done."

"Then we should try it ourselves," he agreed, wrapping an arm around her and earning an adoring look from his wife.

"Will you ever run for representative, Sophia?" asked Nate. "I might throw you a vote, if you convince me of your vision."

"If only the term didn't last five years." She pretended a regretful sigh. "Anyhow, John and I travel far too much to stick around for council meetings on inoculating cows."

"Would you rather have ill cows?" Nate prodded.

John came to Sophia's defense: "Someone must keep the family in touch with the parts of society that haven't yet adopted radical viewpoints. Consider us your ambassadors."

"Ah, John, you are certainly the most diplomatic of us all," Sophia said, glowing.

"Does that make Nate and me the armed forces?" asked Amy. "Are we to do battle on the southern front to keep the Home Office from sending in the militia to quell this democratic uprising?"

"I do still have my uniform," said Nate, grinning.

Caroline shook her head. "None of you need do anything except reply to my letters in a prompt and considerate manner."

Eddie, who was cradling baby Thomas, touched his head to Caroline's. "A little love can go a long way, after all."

Of all the joys Martin could count that day, having his children together, their approval and goodwill flowing as easily as the music from Hamlyn's violin, felt the most precious of all. He reached across the table. "Don't you think it's good form to let the bride and groom hold the baby?"

Baby Thomas sneezed, as if to voice his agreement. Eddie laughed and stood to transfer the baby to Martin's arms. "You must be the expert of these Preston sneezes, sir."

"Those he comes by honestly from his grandmother Lolly," Martin corrected, tucking the baby in the crook of his elbow.

Martha huddled close, leaning in to let Thomas wrap his strong hand around her finger. "You have quite the future ahead of you," she murmured to him. "You spring from so much love, and so many wonderful role models, starting with your grandfather, who is a great and kind man."

"And that's just the beginning of how I would describe Mr. Chow," joked Nate.

Martin smiled in agreement. "What a wonderful future Thomas has. He can learn from two cultures with great histories. He will see the world so differently than I ever did. And he can benefit from all the education we insist on giving him without the burden of knowing he must do anything in particular—except live. Live, and live well, my dear baby Thomas."

"And always do the right thing," added Martha. "But that will come naturally…"

In unison—almost as if they had planned it—Caroline and Eddie and Nate and Amy and Sophia and John all joined her to finish the sentence:

"Because you're a Preston."

And Martin resisted the urge to complicate the sentiment.

AUTHOR'S NOTE

T HANK YOU SO MUCH for reading *The Widower Without a Will,* and (if you've been along for the ride) the whole series! My heart is full writing this author's note because it means we really are at the end of The Prestons. These stories have shaped so much of my life for four years. Through these characters, I have explored idealism, pragmatism, optimism, pessimism, British Regency radicals, and, most of all, beautiful nuances of the heart. It has been a privilege for me, and I hope a satisfying journey for you!

This book touches on the very sensitive theme of suicide. Films and TV shows with this theme usually come with a crisis hotline recommendation. I would like to share this: while writing this novel, my family lost someone dear to us to suicide. The loss is profound. This person probably didn't know they were in my head or my heart, because I did not often interact with them, but they were a gift to the world, and it is worse without them. When I was their age, I experienced suicidal ideation, and I have since learned it is a coping mechanism when my heart is overwhelmed by deep emotions. If you experience suicidal thoughts, please know two things: you matter to so many more people than you think, and there are loved ones, friends, spiritual leaders, and professionals who would like to help you get to the other side. Please, share your pain with someone near and safe to you!

In regard to the historical part of this story, up until 1823, English law dictated that people who died by suicide in England were buried at a crossroads with a stake through their heart. Laws can be archaic, so I looked up news reports from Bath in the early 1800s, and I found references indicating this was still practiced. I never could confirm whether they literally dug up the crossroads, but it seems more likely they used the sides of the intersections so as not to ruin the roads, which is why I decided to use the birch tree as Lucas's marker. Speaking of which, I may have fudged where exactly Martha could get a fantastic, sprawling view of Bath. I hope you'll forgive the artistic license!

When I first began writing The Prestons, I thought the idea of a British lord dreaming of an experimental society was pretty outlandish. Since then, I've discovered there were real utopic societies attempting to redistribute the division of labor in England in the first half of the nineteenth century. Caroline references the Spa Fields community, and Martin is in correspondence with Robert Owen. Both of those are real-life examples, and you can learn more in my research deep dive all about Robert Owen.

Speaking of Lord Preston's vision, at the very end of the novel, he briefly sketches out how the new stewardship council will work. To a modern reader, it may seem unnecessary to declare that the elections will be at regular intervals (every five years) or that the elections will be by secret ballot. In fact, in 1823, those were terms that the average Briton was fighting for in parliamentary reform—not to mention the fight for the franchise. Researching the demands of "radicals" in Regency England continues to highlight for me the fundamental democratic principles that I take for granted and reminds me why it is so important to protect them.

Finally, I would like to note that when I began The Prestons, I chose the very real village of Thatcham as an anchor point so I could find my family on a map of Britain, and I never intended it to become much of a character itself. Any depiction of Thatcham and its villagers in my series is purely my own invention.

For more of the research that went into this book and the rest of the series, unlock my research deep dive archive by subscribing to my free newsletter:

https://bit.ly/katherinegrantresearch

Thank you to everyone who helped me bring this book to fruition! Isabella Kamal and her mother provided great care for Mr. Maulvi. My sister and Abby from Victory Editing gave crucial feedback to hone the story. Sara Israel from Thimble Editorial is my incomparable copyeditor who helps each sentence shine. Julia Gerbach, designer extraordinaire, hand-painted the cover of this book in Adobe Photoshop to age the models to the appropriate age! Thank you also to my Level 9 friend Jisan for lending a character his last name, Zaman.

As always, I thank my wonderful husband, Michael, whose support (in every definition of the word) inspires my writing.

It is an immense pleasure and privilege to publish The Prestons series in completion, with all the themes and detours I envisioned. Thank you for joining me on this journey! The world of Northfield lives on in the Northfield Hall Novellas, including a special anthology coming out in autumn 2026: *Holidays at Northfield Hall*, featuring stories from me, Isabella Kamal, Charlie Lane, Rebecca Paula, and Sri Savita!

PS If you're ever in a house fire, please don't take the extra time to find your cherished belongings. Get out and call the fire department!

About the Author

Katherine Grant writes award-winning Regency Romance novels for the modern reader. Her writing has been recognized by Foreword INDIES Book of the Year Awards, the Next Generation Indie Book Awards, the National Indie Excellence Awards, the Romance Slam Jam Emma Awards, and the Shelf Unbound Indie Book Awards. If you love ballgowns, secret kisses, and social commentary, a book hangover is coming your way.

Katherine also hosts the Historical Romance Sampler podcast! Find out more at www.katherinegrantromance.com

Connect with Katherine on your favorite social media platforms:

instagram.com/katherine_grant_romance/

tiktok.com/@katherinegrantromance

facebook.com/katherinegrantromanceauthor

bookbub.com/authors/katherine-grant

goodreads.com/author/show/19872840.Katherine_Grant

TAKE A TOUR OF NORTHFIELD HALL!

THE PRESTON FAMILY IS famous throughout England for their country seat, where they don't import-export goods, where anyone is welcome who needs a safe place to land, and where the laborers get a share of the estate's profits.

Keep exploring the world of Northfield Hall with an estate map and a 3-minute virtual tour of the great house!

Unlock the tour by subscribing to my newsletter:

https://bit.ly/northfieldhall

MORE FROM KATHERINE GRANT

Catch up on The Prestons series:

The Baron Without Blame – A Prequel Novella
He may not know her name, but that won't stop him from proposing a fake engagement...

The Viscount Without Virtue – Book 2
When she discovers her family's enemy is hiding in plain sight, what choice does a lady have but to seduce him?

The Governess Without Guilt – Book 3

One bored governess, one handsome doctor, and unchaperoned nighttime activities. What could possibly go wrong?

The Charmer Without a Cause – Book 4
Everyone knows that a happy marriage begins with a lot of money and one good lie...

The Sailor Without a Sweetheart – Book 5
Is love worth giving a second chance?

The Countess Without Conviction – Book 6/A Related Novella
Is Ellen and Max's marriage strong enough to weather this storm?

The Miss Without a Mister – Book 7
Two hearts, one vow, and a world built to keep them apart. Can true love conquer all, or is this romance destined for heartbreak?

The Widower Without a Will – Book 8
This secret love affair risks nothing except his legacy—and her heart.

Explore the world of Northfield Hall:

The Hellion of Drury Lane
Behind the scenes, drama cuts both ways.

It's In Her Kiss

No good deed goes unkissed...

Three Nights With Her Husband

On this road trip, one bed is never enough...

Letters to Her Love

They are writing their love story one letter at a time...

In The Wide Open Light

She is willing to fight for reform, but will she fight for the man she loves?

Her Perfect Pirate

On this pirate ship, their fake marriage isn't meant to last...

Don't miss my first series, The Countess Chronicles:

The Ideal Countess – Book 1

Will a garden scandal lead to a duel at dawn, or happily ever after?

New Year's Masquerade – Book 1.5

With one night left of freedom, will Bernard choose to obey duty or follow his heart?

The Duchess Wager – Book 2
Will the duke lose the bet or his heart?

The Husband Plot – Book 3
What could go wrong when you marry a perfect stranger?

THANKS FOR READING!

I AM SO GRATEFUL you joined me on this journey back in time. If you enjoyed it, please consider leaving a rating or review on your ebook retailer, Goodreads, or wherever else you talk about books!

Until next time...